The Chandana Tree

A Novel by

Norm Kohn

PublishAmerica
Baltimore

First printing

This book is a work of fiction. Names, characters, places and incidents are products of the author's imagination and are used fictitiously. Any resemblance to actual events, locales or persons, living or dead is purely coincidental.

ISBN: 1-4137-6264-6
PUBLISHED BY PUBLISHAMERICA, LLLP
www.publishamerica.com
Baltimore

Printed in the United States of America

For Kathy, Kumi, Yuu and Mineaki

Within the forest of the poisonous Errand trees only Errand trees are said to grow, but not the fragrant Chandana. It is a miracle if a Chandana tree grows in an Errand forest.
                                                    -Shakyamuni Buddha

ACKNOWLEDGMENTS

On the shoulders of the muse sit many angels without whom her work would be for naught. Among that host to whom I am most grateful: My wife, Kathy, for her unremitting support and keen editorial eye; Terry Kay, for his inspiration, patient mentoring and tireless commitment to the cause; Jim Cypher, Hilda Brucker and Jeanne Jacobson, for their guidance through the literary thicket; Azusa Kuwano, my sensei and resident expert on all things Japanese; Coleman Breland, who never tired of listening, reading and prodding; Steven Petsch, master photographer, whose images of Japan remain a constant joy, and the legion of family and friends who by their presence have made this story their own.

Quotation from the Buddha is from *The Teaching of Buddha* courtesy of Bukkyô Dendô Kyôkai (Society for the Promotion of Buddhism), Tokyo, Japan.

CHAPTER 1

The first message appeared at 10:50 P.M. at thirty-one thousand feet somewhere over the Nevada desert.

An appealing ass
Even so the tiger flees
Fearless courage lost

was neatly typed just below the last line of his story synopsis.

Jonathan stared in disbelief at the glowing computer screen propped in his lap. He read the cryptic lines a second time and a wet chill crept in under his stressed denim collar. He hesitated, then moved the cursor to the *Explorer* icon and punched into the file tree. He found *My Documents*, opened the *Lotus Matrix* file and studied the dated entry. The document had been last modified on Friday at 2:32 P.M. That was two hours before he boarded the flight for L.A.

The damp, short hairs on the back of his neck shivered. *Damn,* he thought. *How could that be? I was working on the machine at 2:30.* He fought off the drowning sensation, thought back to Friday and visualized his cubicle at SatCom.

It was one of a maze of impersonal gray fabric warrens furnished in standard issue walnut and stainless steel. The one civilizing element in his space was a battered antique cobbler's bench he used as a side table.

He had been packing to leave and the place was a mess, but he could see the gray case of the closed laptop sitting right on the corner of his desk next to the phone, the Deco clock, the kanji mouse pad and the picture of Hemingway holding his catnip mouse. Earlier, he had run out for a quick lunch, but he had returned and was pounding away on the systems brochure by 12:30.

He had worked until 3:15, then printed it out and stepped into Stanley's office with the final draft. The Prince of Procrastination had been in the midst of an intense telephone conversation, so Jonathan had laid the copy on his desk and was back in his chair at 3:30.

That was it. He had been away from his desk a few minutes at lunch and the five minutes it took to get in and out of Stanley's office. Besides, the file had been changed at 2:32 when he was actually working on the machine.

He refocused on the computer screen and the short hairs went electric. *Goddamn, that's impossible. I was alone. How could anybody enter a message while I was typing?* He pushed his glasses up on his forehead, sagged back in the seat and closed his eyes. *I'm getting too old for this*, he thought. *Only two days in La La Land and I'm already in the Twilight Zone.*

The atmosphere in the 757's cabin suddenly felt restrictive. Jonathan fumbled for his air vent and twisted it open. He sucked in a cool, deep breath and tried to visualize a peaceful purple lagoon, but all he got for his efforts was the rush hour at an ozone-soaked Marina del Rey and a blinking neon sign that reminded him that some cyber-spook was messing around with his head.

The flight into LAX had been uneventful, which was a blessing. The four hours had given him a chance to catch his breath after the rush hour dash to the airport and time to make the mental transition from Atlanta to Hollywood.

It was his first time in L.A. since Landon's invitation to join the Abracadabra Project. He liked the group's name. It was one of the reasons he was even willing to consider the offer. Compared to the staid, puckered-up corporate culture at SatCom, it conjured up images of free falling in Never Never Land.

The thought of stepping outside the company safety net and

throwing in with a bunch of the "Lost Boys" floating around at the end of a rainbow was unsettling, but Margo had checked his planetary alignments and said the timing looked promising. Besides, she had pointed out, the offer was coming at a good time, and he had to admit she had a point. SatCom was rife with merger paranoia, and Stanley's usual state of denial had only aggravated the insecurity and rumors flying around the communications department. It was beginning to look like the walls of his sanctuary might be crumbling.

From the outset, the merger plans emanating from the executive suite had not been popular with middle management and staff—too many over-built homes and SUVs hung in the balance. Accordingly, one rumor had it that, if the deal went through, every guy in the food chain up to senior management was going to go down and, en masse, pee on the chairman's statue in the SatCom lobby. Jonathan had been impressed. It was one of the few creative ideas that had come out of corporate in the five years he had been there.

So, when Landon called and offered him the slot with Abracadabra, and Margo gazed into the stars and said go for it, he bit the bullet, sucked up the tattered remains of his confidence, took a day of vacation, and caught a plane into what he feared might be a setting sun.

Fenton Longstreet locked the aging van, fed the parking meter, then crossed the street toward a tree-shaded row of trendy shops and restaurants. He squeezed between two decorative iron benches, dodged an attractive blond in black spandex running her Doberman, and turned into the Online Café.

He reached for the doorknob and caught a glimpse of himself in the storefront window. The image staring back had a one-day growth of rusty beard, worn jeans, dirty sneakers and black sweatshirt topped off with a rumpled Harris Tweed sport coat. *Jesus, that picture is the story of my life,* he thought. It was a long way from the cushy cul-de-sac, the Porsche, the Gucci loafers, and the Commerce Club by way of too much bourbon and not enough Coke.

The Harris Tweed was the last remaining memento of his brief days of glory, and even though it was tired and frayed, he could not let it go. Mary Beth had gotten all the rest. Thank God he'd had the coat on when she switched the locks. Theirs had been a wheel-of-fortune relationship, but, as the shadow in the window reminded him, he sure as hell was nobody's prize. *Oh, well, screw it,* he thought, as he turned the knob and stepped into the café.

The room Fenton entered was a fusion of fifties decor and millennium technology that he found oddly comforting. Soda-fountain tables and chairs were scattered around the room, and computer stations and high-speed connections lined the walls creating, on the one hand, areas of intimate conversation and, on the other, digital windows of interpersonal anonymity. He saw it as a microcosm of contemporary life and it suited his needs perfectly.

After the divorce eighteen months ago, and his entry into the program, he had severed ties with friends and family, walked away from the firm, and dropped out. The pain and humiliation had simply been too great. He had needed time, but more than that, he needed space to begin to reassemble his life. That's when he packed all his belongings into the modified van and started moving around from one campground and vacant lot to another.

When he needed to communicate, he had used pay phones, until six months ago when he discovered the Online Café. The café had become his island in the stream—a place for managed conversation and controlled on-line access to the world and those very few friendships he had chosen to re-establish. With e-mail he could be contacted, but not located. He decided when to pick up his messages and *if* he would return them. It was a safe way to re-enter the flow, and at the same time, stay out of reach. Fenton Longstreet was slowly working his way back to shore.

"Ah, Mr. Longstreet, AKA Junkyard Dog, I presume." He was greeted by the smiling, middle-aged, ex-corporate sysop behind the counter. "Log in and make yourself at home. What can I get for you?"

"Hi, Vincent." Fenton leaned on the counter and studied the menu on the wall. "How about a corned beef on rye and cup of coffee."

"No espresso?" Vincent's voice reflected a hint of disapproval. Fenton smiled. "Just plain old Colombian, black."

"You're the one who has to drink it," Vincent admonished, and entered the order into the electronic cash register. "Need a card?"

Fenton fished a maroon plastic card with the café's logo out of his wallet. "No, I've still got plenty of time on this one. Thanks though."

"Don't mention it. That'll be seven-fifty."

Fenton counted out a five and four ones. "Keep the change. How's business?"

Vincent put the cash in the drawer and turned to a coffee urn. His demeanor brightened. "Couldn't be better. We ran a special last weekend and had surfers standing in line." He filled a coffee mug and slid it across the counter. "Sandwich'll be up in a minute."

"Thanks. I'll be over on R2D2."

"I'll bring it over. Have a good trip."

Fenton nodded, picked up the coffee mug and a napkin and crossed the room to the bank of computer stations lining the wall. He sat down in front of a machine identified as R2D2 by the nameplate on the wall above the monitor. To his right was C-3PO and on his left was the Death Star piloted by a kid with green hair. It was a whimsical touch that would have been lost on him six months ago. He took the maroon plastic card and pulled it through the card reader attached to the counter next to the keyboard, then booted the machine and logged on to: *onlinecafe.com*.

As soon as the web page loaded, he clicked on the e-mail button and typed in his ID: *junkdog*. Then he punched in his password: *litigate*, and felt a warm, visceral surge. *Shit*. He sighed. *The old dog still has teeth. I've got to get rid of that damned password*. But it was like the Harris Tweed: a remnant from the past he had not been able to cast off.

When the window opened, he saw that he had one new piece of mail from: *jlseagull. Subject: the eagle has landed*.

Ah, the prodigal has returned from the Promised Land, he thought. He took a sip of coffee, opened the message and scrolled down to the text.

Hey Fent,
Just got in from L.A. Good trip, although I'm still in a time warp. But something strange happened on the way back, and we need to talk. How about dinner at Sakana Ya? You pick the day and time and I'll be there. Look forward to seeing your raggedy ass.
Jonathan

Strange sounds interesting, Fenton thought. He clicked on the reply button and typed:

hi asshole,
glad ur home. would enjoy something a little strange. see u tomorrow night—sakanna ya at 6:30. hasta la vista.
Ps—is she into black leather or feather boas?

Fenton reread his reply, smiled and hit *Send*.

CHAPTER 2

The light filtering through the window created a soft, transcendental wash that burnished the comfortable sitting room with an intimate patina.

Margo was convinced that it entered the room in waveform, only to crystallize into a counterpoint of particle and wave when it encountered the mist of incense and hushed New Age music awaiting its arrival. She had long suspected there was a direct connection between sound and optical wave lengths that, when fine-tuned with the other physical senses, had a direct effect on the frequencies that formed the human body and psyche.

As Margo saw it, life was a dance created simultaneously on the cosmic and personal scale from a shared score of those most intimate vibrational yearnings. Everyone danced. It was just that few could hear the music clearly enough to follow its lead. That was Margo's gift. Or her curse, depending on how she chose to look at it. Either way, she had "it," and there wasn't much she could do but make the best of what she thought at times was an uncertain blessing.

Margo not only heard the music and saw the dancers, she understood and could interpret the choreography, but she wasn't a fortune cookie. The times she saw the next act waiting in the wings Margo kept to herself. She wasn't in the business of shuffling cards and quick psychic fixes. She saw herself as a guide, not a soothsayer. She was a spiritual tuning fork—a cross between a shrink, an artist's model and a dancing Wu Li Master. It was the years spent naked in art classes and conjuring recreation on cruise ships that gave her psychic revelations the salt of credibility, and provided a faithful list of clients who would die for her.

Margo checked her watch then ran her finger down the list of appointments in the book that lay open before her on the antique breakfront she used as a desk. It had been a busy day. Venus was still in conjunction with Mars, and the planetary tension was creating an unusually crowded schedule. *It's going to be a long week,* she thought. But today was almost a wrap, just her 5:30 to go. She had ten minutes.

She pondered the last entry. Jennifer Mitford was a new client. She had called late Friday afternoon hoping to get an early week appointment. Margo had worked her in because she said she was a friend of Jonathan's, and any friend of Jonathan's got special treatment. She closed her eyes, breathed deeply and absorbed the name into her mind's eye. She let it float for thirty seconds, then closed the appointment book, walked to the window and pulled back the curtain. A light rain had started to fall, transforming the light waves and turning the room into liquid silver. She turned to a heart-shaped mirror on the wall and admired the luminosity of her jade green eyes. Then she unbuttoned the top button of her blouse and ran her hands through her flame red hair. Margo studied her reflection and smiled. It was show time at the cosmic café.

Twenty-five hundred miles away, across the great American cultural divide, a cell phone rang. Landon Tarkenton pulled himself easily out of the swimming pool, dried his hands with a thick terry towel, picked up the phone and pressed the receive button.

"Landon here," he spoke into the miniscule handset, while he toweled the tight curls of his pepper-gray hair with his free hand.

A smile lit up his still damp face. "Hello, my man. Are you back in the land of button-up?"

He spread the towel over a pool lounge and settled comfortably into it.

"Glad you did. It was great to have you here." He paused, and a film of concern tightened his tanned face.

"Jon, I meant what I said. It doesn't make any difference that you're the only out-of-towner. That's the whole point. We need a different spirit; besides, everybody is crazy about you. In fact, my partner, Peter Finch, called this morning and said how great it was to hear somebody say yonder and y'all again. And he wasn't being facetious. He's been out of Mississippi and into studio-speak for so long he's damn near forgotten how to talk, much less write. That's the reason for this exercise. I'm trying to stir the creative pot. Besides, I wouldn't have called you if I didn't think you are one of the most talented writers I know."

The sun drilled a hole through the high smog over Studio City, showering the pool with dazzling filings of light. Shadows that had been indistinct suddenly snapped into focus, and the water sparkled like a Tahitian lagoon. It was another Southern California special effect courtesy of Mother Nature, and Landon made a mental note of it in his memory bank of cinematic illusions.

He nodded. "Uh-huh, absolutely, you can take it to the bank." He sat up, turned to a poolside table and stirred a pitcher of lemonade, then carefully poured a drink.

"Anything you can write I can get on the air." He leaned forward, as if focusing on someone in front of him.

"And when I say anything, Jon, I mean anything," he said intently, totally fixed in the moment, the drink halfway to his mouth.

"Great, Jon. Glad you feel that way, Amigo."

The tension broke.

"Then I'll hear from you by the end of the week."

He lay back in the lounge and the glass finally made it to his lips. He sipped slowly and listened for a minute longer, then nodded.

"Sayonara."

He pressed the off button with his thumb, placed the phone on the table, and picked up a copy of *The Hollywood Reporter*.

Damn, he thought, *it's always one step at a time.*

Jonathan hung up the phone and stared out the window. A light rain was falling, and from his eighth-story office window he could see the traffic backing up on I-285. *Landon hasn't changed,* he thought: *still confident, unfailingly supportive and always in control.*

He remembered the day Landon announced he was leaving the agency. It caught the entire Atlanta advertising community by surprise. Everyone knew Landon liked to fool around with film, but nobody imagined that the star creative director of the hottest shop in town would up and trash his career for an uncertain future in Tinseltown. Jonathan had been amazed by the audacity of the move. The idea of walking away from success and leaping into the unknown held the potential of myth and, true to form, after a series of successful cop and doc shows, Landon Tarkington had become a player in Hollywood and a legend in his home town.

The fact that Landon had given Jonathan his first creative job had become a defining part of Jonathan's mythology, and the battle ribbons they had won in the advertising wars were among his most prized memories. Memories that, in the dark times to come, had kept his creative spark smoldering even after the candle had been smothered.

Jonathan watched the congested traffic creeping along on the rain-slick highway far below and wondered if history might be repeating itself. Perhaps some karmic—He was interrupted by the intrusive ring of his telephone. He pulled himself out of his reverie and picked up the handset.

"Hi, Jennifer, God, is it that late?" he said in surprise. "No, we're all caught up. You can go."

He looked at the Deco clock. "Sure, you too. Have a nice evening."

Damn, he thought, *I've got to get out of here if I'm going to get home, feed Hemingway, and meet Fent by 6:30.* He hurriedly cleaned off his desk, grabbed his coat from the rack behind him and tugged it on while he slid the closed laptop computer into its bag. He threw the strap over his shoulder and started for the elevator, then remembered the rain and went back for his umbrella. *Always prepared, always the boy scout,* he thought.

18

Margo studied the young woman seated before her. She was pretty in a winsome way. Her strawberry hair fell in ringlets about her face and brushed her shoulders when she moved her head. *She has good bone structure,* Margo observed. The high, sculpted cheekbones were accented by a carefully drawn, slightly upturned, almost artful nose. But it was the woman's eyes that held Margo. Their slight angle suggested a tantalizing hint of the east. Then the elixir of light, music and incense dissolved their blue-gray veil and revealed a depth of passion, strength, sadness and vulnerability that Margo found enormously seductive.

"Jennifer is a lovely name," she said softly as Jennifer's eyes released her.

"Thank you. It was my father's choice." The barest hint of the sadness touched the corners of her lips.

"Your father has good taste," Margo said.

"Yes, he did. He died when I was five."

How did I miss that? Margo thought. "I'm sorry. That's very young," she said gently.

"I know. I've missed him very much." She hesitated, lost in her memories. "But, it was a long time ago."

Margo nodded. "Yes, it was." She paused. "Why have you come to me?" she asked.

Jennifer slipped back into the present. "I understand you teach people to dance," she answered.

CHAPTER 3

Jonathan checked his watch as he passed Fenton's van in the rain-splashed parking lot. *Only ten minutes late. Not too bad,* he thought, *considering the pile-up on I-285, and the bumper-to-bumper traffic on the cross-town surface streets.* He stopped under the awning of the softly lit Japanese restaurant and closed his umbrella. *Fent will already have a table,* he thought as he stepped into the small shoji-paper and oak waiting area.

"Ah, *konban wa,* Jonathan-*san.*" An attractive hostess in a bright kimono greeted him.

Jonathan bowed slightly. "*Konban wa, Mishi-san,*" he replied.

She returned his bow. "*Kyo wa tenki ga warui desu ne.*"

Jonathan nodded'. "Yes, it's a terrible night. Is Mr. Longstreet already here?"

Mishi smiled. "Yes, he's back this way." She turned toward the gently illuminated dining room.

Fenton was studying the menu as they approached the table.

"Longstreet-*san,* your guest has arrived," Mishi announced in her lyrical voice. "Jonathan-*san,* what would you like to drink?"

"Green tea, thank you, Mishi-*san.*" He pulled out a chair opposite Fenton and sat down.

"Yuko-*san* will be serving you tonight. Enjoy your dinner, gentlemen." With that, Mishi bowed one final time and turned away.

Fenton watched her flutter back to her station at the door.

Jonathan read his look and chuckled. "She'll break your red-neck heart, Fenton-*san,*" he admonished.

Before Fenton could reply, a smiling, dark-eyed waitress dressed in a blue and white *yukata* and red sash appeared at their table with a pot of green tea and two cups.

"Hi, Jonathan, how goes it?" she asked.

"I'm doing well, Yuko. How about you?"

"Fine, thank you." She put the tea on the table and took an order pad and pencil from her sash. "You gentlemen ready to order?"

Jonathan had not opened his menu, but he didn't have to; he knew it by heart. "I am. How about you, Fent?"

"Go ahead, I'm almost there." He ran his finger slowly down the list of items.

"I'd like some hot noodles. *Kitsune soba*," Jonathan said, and handed her his menu.

She noted it down and smiled at Fenton.

"I need beef. I'll go with *sukiyaki*."

Yuko nodded approvingly. "Good choice for a rainy night. Would you care for an appetizer?"

Jonathan looked at Fenton. "Sure, how about some sushi. I'll have *unagi*. Fent?"

Fenton grimaced. "No matter how you spell it, *u-n-a-g-i* or e-e-l, it's a snake." He smiled apologetically at Yuko. "One California roll."

Yuko bowed slightly and closed her pad. "Enjoy your tea. I'll be back with your sushi in a minute."

When she had gone, Jonathan poured a cup of tea and passed it to Fenton, then poured one for himself. "It's really not a snake, you know."

"I know."

Jonathan smiled and sat back. "How are you doing, my friend?" he asked.

Fenton warmed his hands over the steaming teacup. "Not too bad for a gypsy."

"How much longer are you planning to live out of dumpsters?" Jonathan asked.

Fenton cautiously sipped his tea and considered the question.

"Dumpsters have gotten a bad rap, and you forget I have a microwave." Then his shoulders sagged. "But, to answer your question, counselor, I don't know." He looked up at Jonathan. "How much longer are you going to wander in the corporate wilderness?" His fingers did the math. "What's it been, five years now?"

As Fenton spoke, Jonathan felt a sudden, remorseless surge of dark waves lift, then overwhelm him. He took a deep breath and stared into the tea as if, through some ancient herbal magic, it might bear him up one more time and expel the inexorable pain that threatened to suck him under.

"Hey, guys. Why so glum?" Yuko was standing beside the table with their sushi. She looked anxiously from one to the other. "Are you okay?" she asked tentatively.

"Yuko." Jonathan slowly exhaled. "You're an angel of mercy." The waves crested and were gone as stealthily as they had come. He looked at Fenton. "Just chasing old dogs."

Yuko laughed uncertainly. "I don't understand angels and old dogs." Then her face brightened. "But this is very good sushi." She put the order on the table. "Care for more tea?"

"That would be great," Jonathan replied.

Yuko appeared relieved. "Okay. Be right back. Enjoy your sushi."

After she left, Fenton poured some soy sauce and slowly mixed it with wasabi. "I'm sorry I kicked that dog, Jonathan. I was way out of line."

"No, Fent, it's okay. I went there first; besides," Jonathan smiled ruefully, "I need someone other than Margo kicking my ass."

Their eyes met and Jonathan slowly raised his cup of tea. "*Kanpai*. To two lost dogs."

An easy grin creased Fenton's face and he lifted his cup. "Make that two lost souls."

Jonathan's smile broadened. "To two lost souls," he seconded.

They drained their cups and put them on the table.

"And now, would you like to tell me what's going on?" Fenton pushed his empty cup across the table. "Is the lady into black leather or feather boas?"

Jonathan poured the remaining tea, then sat back. "I don't know, Fent. I haven't met her."

"So, it is a woman?"

Jonathan skipped a beat. "Well, damn, I hope so."

"Now, you're getting weird."

"And I have a feeling it's only the beginning," Jonathan said uneasily. Then he recounted the appearance of the mysterious message on his computer. While he talked, Fenton made notes on a napkin.

When Jonathan had finished, Fenton was silent while he studied the three lines he had recorded. "This has the feel of a Haiku poem."

Jonathan nodded. "Yeah, I noticed."

Fenton read the message again, then slowly drew a line under *the tiger* and turned the paper toward Jonathan. "Is this who I think it is?"

Jonathan leaned forward and rested wearily on the table. He had understood its meaning the instant the words first appeared in the dark night of the Nevada sky.

"I'm afraid it is, Fent." He paused as he recalled his initial shock. "I was born in 1962, the Japanese year of the tiger. I'm the tiger."

Fenton stared at Jonathan for a moment, then retrieved the napkin and carefully drew a box around *flees, fearless courage lost.*

"Nice ass, tigers and lost dogs aside, Jonathan, whoever sent this thing is hitting pretty close to home."

Jonathan sighed. "A little too close, Fent."

Fenton folded the napkin, slipped it into his jacket pocket and leaned back, lost in thought, while Yuko placed their dinner on the table and removed the empty sushi plate.

When she was gone, he took the message out and unfolded it. "I don't understand how somebody could put this on your computer at the exact time you were working on it."

"And not just anywhere on the computer, but in the *Lotus Matrix* file. Someone knows my work habits well enough to know that I couldn't miss it there."

Fenton stirred his *sukiyaki*. "Do you normally work on your laptop at the office?"

"Yes and no. Usually I use the desktop machine. When I take work home on the laptop, I transfer it back to the desktop the next morning. But on Friday I didn't bother to make the transfer, since I was leaving early for L.A. and wanted to take some work with me. So I worked on the laptop most of the day."

"And with the exception of going to lunch and stepping into Stanley's office it was with you the whole day?" Fenton asked.

"Every minute."

"Was anyone in your cubicle at lunch?"

"I asked Mildred, our secretary. She sits two stations down from me. With the exception of Jennifer Mitford dropping off a layout and picking up some copy, she didn't see anyone in my space. And, she ate lunch at her desk."

"What about Mildred?"

Jonathan laughed. "Mildred is old enough to be my mother."

Fenton shrugged. "So was Mrs. Robinson."

Jonathan shook his head. "Not Mildred. We call her Mother Goose. She thinks the department is her shoe."

"All right, but she's on the list." He made a note. "Who's Jennifer Mitford?"

"The copywriter I work with."

Fenton jotted her name down. "What about your e-mail?"

"I usually use the laptop for personal mail, but it wasn't connected so I used the desktop."

"I'd be careful about that if I were you. Your desktop is hard-wired into the corporate system. With Abracadabra, and some of the stuff we kick back and forth, and now this...."

Jonathan pondered the consequences of the company stumbling onto his private life, especially Abracadabra. "Yeah, Fent, you're right. I'll be more careful."

Fenton nodded. "Okay. So it couldn't have been downloaded. Have there been any more messages?"

"There wasn't anything this morning, but I haven't checked it since then," Jonathan answered.

"But you had it at work?"

Jonathan nodded. "Right on my desk in its usual place."

"Do you have it with you now? I'd like to see that message."

"Sure, it's in the car. I'll run out and get it." Jonathan put his chopsticks down and pushed his chair back.

Fenton hunched forward. "I hate to even mention it, Jonathan, because this could be nothing more than an elaborate joke, but in my natural state of prosecutorial paranoia, I'm seeing reruns of *Play Misty For Me*. Someone has done their homework. Do you know anybody who might want to keep tabs on you?"

Jonathan hesitated by the table and a note of concern entered his voice. "Yeah, Fent, I thought of that too, and no, I don't." The short hairs twitched. "The last thing I need is a stalker in my life."

Fenton looked up with a half-serious expression. "Depending on the stalker, that might be exactly what you need." He leaned back. "Better look both ways and behind you when you cross the parking lot."

"Thanks for the comforting thought," Jonathan said, and headed for the door.

Margo sat on the earth-colored sofa and looked out the window at the night rain. She hadn't moved since Jennifer left. She floated on the incense and the music, watching the rain and listening to her heart and her sixth sense. Something was stirring on the cosmic breeze, but it was just out of reach, just beginning to rustle her psychic leaves. She knew from experience that it was too soon to draw any conclusions or even venture a guess. Only time would tell if she should batten down the hatches or dance in the rain, but she suspected that the answer lay somewhere in the alluring, blue-gray eyes of the woman who had just left.

A distant flash of lightning traced across the sky followed by a roll of thunder so muted that she momentarily mistook it for the music. Point and counterpoint, yin and yang, spirit and flesh— contrasting energies followed the path the lightning etched in her mind. *The wind and the surf are definitely up,* she thought, *and I must be careful to catch the right wave.*

Margo surfed the metaphysical isobar for a moment longer, then walked over to the breakfront and picked up her appointment calendar. She would see Jennifer again on Wednesday, and they would get down to serious work. She turned the page back to Tuesday and was pleased to see that Jonathan was her five o'clock.

Ten minutes later, as Margo locked the door of her office and stepped out into the rain, Jonathan returned to the table at Sakana Ya with a gym bag. He unzipped it and pulled out a laptop computer.

Fenton pushed the remnants of the finished meal out of the way. "Nice computer bag."

"My anti-corporate statement. Thought you'd like it," Jonathan replied and booted up. When the desktop screen loaded, he moved the cursor toward the *My Documents* shortcut icon. He never got there. "Oh, holy shit," he exclaimed in a hoarse whisper.

Fenton looked up in surprise. "What is it?" He got up and came around the table where he could see the screen over Jonathan's shoulder.

"Look at this." On the screen, next to the *My Documents Folder,* was a new file titled *Black Leather & Feather Boas.*

CHAPTER 4

I rise from the water nearly naked,
numb, with only my head left alive.
The wind works as though it has fingers,
unbuttoning its way, sapping my warmth
like a half-crazed lover.

The snow consumes me. Its white teeth snap
at my flesh, tearing, twisting, slashing,
devouring even the damp life-breath caught still
warm in my nostrils—

Jonathan woke up in a cold sweat. He lay perfectly still and stared at the ceiling for two feverish minutes as the last verse of the poem wound down in his mind, then he kicked the covers off, swung his feet to the floor and braced on the edge of the bed. The bedside clock blinked off the seconds past 4:22 A.M. He stared at the digital readout for another thirty seconds, then stumbled into the bathroom, soaked a washcloth with cold water and held it against his face.

The damp cloth cooled his skin but did nothing to calm the boiling waves crashing in his mind. He peered at the faceless shape in the mirror for a minute before feeling his way back into the dark bedroom. *Goddamn,* he thought, *what kicked that off? It's been six months since the last dream. Thank God I'm seeing Margo today.* He sighed, sat down on the bed and looked at the clock: 4:27 and change. *I'll never get back to sleep.*

The cerebral surf was settling down, but it needed some help. 4:29. He picked up the TV remote from the bedside table and punched power, then 17 for WTBS, and a sudden feeling of loneliness swept over him. He looked at the clock and calculated the time difference. *It will be almost 5:30 and they should be having drinks,* he thought. He picked up the telephone handset and dialed the international number for Japan as the visual static on the TV screen restructured itself into the opening titles for Gomer Pyle.

Three miles away, in a modest loft apartment, Jennifer Mitford sat bolt upright in bed. She was in survival mode on red alert. She couldn't breathe, and her locked muscles wouldn't let her move. Her early warning system had shut down all body functions except for her sensory alarms, which were on overload, scanning for unknown or unexplained variations in the patterns that formed the normal fabric of the night.

After what seemed an eternity with no blips on the danger screen, she took a hesitant breath, screwed up her courage and slipped slowly out of bed. It was a scenario she had played out several times since David had attempted to force his way into the apartment, and it was beginning to rattle her. She picked up a small canister of mace from the shelf of her bedside table and edged down the short hall, past the kitchen and into the living room.

From where she stood behind a large potted plant, she could see the entire space. The only points of entry were the front door to her left, the sliding glass doors onto the deck, and the window to her right. The light from the street lamp in the parking lot filtered across the living room, illuminating a small sofa, an Oriental rug, a single chair, and a dining room table with a laptop computer sitting open on it. There wasn't a sound and, except for the wind stirring in a tree by the window, there was no movement. She scanned the room again. There was no evidence of forced entry; everything was just as it should be—tidy and in its place.

Jennifer felt the muscles in her shoulders start to relax. *Must have been a dream,* she thought, as she cautiously crossed the room to the window and looked out over the walled, carefully tended plot behind the building.

She was sure she hadn't imagined the shadowy figure standing in the darkness near the corner of her garden two nights before. But tonight there was no fleeting apparition lurking among the late hydrangeas and asters, waiting to send shivers crawling up her spine.

She examined the shadows once more; then, when she was satisfied they concealed no threat, she turned and followed the light of the bed table clock back to her bedroom. *God, it's 4:35,* she thought; *I'm so wired I'll never get back to sleep. Maybe I can just numb-out.*

Jennifer piled her pillows against the headboard and collapsed on the bed. She stared into the darkness, then reached over to the bedside table and picked up the TV remote. She fingered the buttons, and five seconds later the dense grin of Gomer Pyle filled the screen.

Jonathan freely admitted that his teenage years growing up in Japan were the most memorable of his life. The five years spent in Yokosuka at the southern end of Tokyo Bay came toward the end of his father's career in the Navy. He considered himself lucky, for as he saw it, he was able to blend the best of East and West. While many of his friends seemed indifferent to their surroundings, he had decided that, in a previous life, he must have been a shogun or even a geisha. He was one of the few who had made the effort to learn the language.

It was here that his father taught him to sail, and among his fondest memories were the afternoons they slipped away together and explored the nearby islands in their small sailboat.

When he needed a break from the hustle of the American high school activities on the base, he would hike up a trail that led from their home to a hidden grotto, where he had discovered a large and, he was sure, very ancient Buddha. There he would rest in the cool, translucent shadow of his enigmatic and impenetrable host, look out over the polished jade bay, and listen for the voices of the *kami* in the sighing of the wind. The gods never spoke, but in the wisdom of their silence and the stillness of the Buddha, he unconsciously absorbed a center point and space that he would soon discover was largely missing in the West.

It was culture shock when his father was reassigned to the Pentagon and the family moved back to the States. But a life of moving around the world, and the time spent in the shadow of the Buddha, had given him the ability to adjust quickly to new situations. So, after a brief withdrawal period, he settled into college life at the University of Georgia in Athens, the town where he was born. Two years later, Jonathan's father retired and accepted a position representing a Japanese company that did contract work for the Navy at the Yokosuka shipyard, and the door to Japan opened again.

The images of those days played out for Jonathan as he listened to the electronic beeps of his call flashing through space to a ground station half a world away. There was a brief hesitation and then the sound of a phone ringing, followed by a familiar voice.

"*Moshi, moshi.*"

"Hi, Mom, it's me."

"Why, Jonathan, what a pleasant surprise." She hesitated, and he knew she was figuring the time.

"My, you're up awfully early." There was another slight pause, and a note of concern entered her voice. "There's nothing wrong is there?"

Jonathan relaxed. *God, that's just what he needed to hear. How he loved this woman.*

"No, Mom. I just woke up and couldn't get back to sleep, so I thought I'd call and see how you and Dad are doing."

Her voice brightened. "Oh, you know us, busy as can be. Your father is out with Mr. Takamoto at a business meeting, so I'm having a couple of friends over for the evening." She paused again, and a remnant of concern crept back into her voice. "How about you? Have you been out lately?"

Jonathan lay back on the bed. He knew exactly what she was thinking, and he hated to disappoint her.

"No, Mom. No new women on the horizon, but Hemingway is doing fine."

"I know I shouldn't push, but I worry about you being alone. After all, it has been five years."

Tonight she can push all she wants, Jonathan thought. He knew the concern came from a warm and gentle heart, and he found it reassuring and comforting.

"Thanks, Mom, but I'm okay, honest," he replied.

They chatted for another ten minutes then said their good-byes just as Sergeant Carter caught Gomer sneaking out of the barracks.

In Jennifer's darkened bedroom Gomer stumbled, and fell down the barracks steps with Sergeant Carter in hot pursuit, accompanied by a burst of muted sound-track laughter. But Jennifer couldn't see or hear. She had fallen asleep with the remote control in her hand.

Across town, in a half-empty campground, Fenton rolled over and checked his watch. *Shit, it's only 5:30,* he thought. He pulled back the window curtain and looked out into a slash pine thicket. A lone mercury vapor lamp illuminated the office fifty yards away with its surreal metallic glow, while beyond the trees dawn was starting to unzip the dark skin of the night. He closed the curtain and stretched out in the bed. He knew it would be futile to attempt sleep, so he crawled out from between the sheets, put a coffeepot on the stove, and felt his way across the peeling linoleum floor into the miniature bathroom.

Fifteen minutes later he had folded up the bed and was sitting at a small dining table, fortified with a cup of coffee and a bagel, and armed with a legal pad and ball point pen. He doodled as the coffee pumped caffeine into his complaining vascular system.

Doodling was as close as Fenton got to his subconscious. He was naturally suspicious of esoteric exercises that promised insights not readily available by analytic deduction. He viewed reality as an

31

elegant structure of definable events and systems that could be observed, defined, categorized, and then manipulated by the power of rational thought and action.

Margo, with her other-planetary spiritual meanderings, totally dumbfounded him; however, he confessed a deep respect and secret admiration for the seemingly irrational process by which Jonathan went about solving problems and translating reality into lucid and, occasionally, breathtaking word pictures. Fenton would never be caught dead mind-surfing in the lotus position, so he doodled, which, ironically, opened the doors to those suspect levels of perception in ways he could never admit.

This morning he drew strings of arrows converging on a thin rectangular shape that he had decorated with an open lid and several knobs. He stopped drawing and pondered the image, then carefully delineated on the inside of the lid the curving lines of a woman's face and nude torso. He admired his work, then drew a black mask on the face and a question mark on her ample bosom. He took a sip of coffee and a bite of bagel and thought back to the night before, when the mysterious *Black Leather & Feather Boas* file had appeared on Jonathan's computer screen.

They had stared at the icon for a full five seconds before Jonathan found his voice. "I'll be damned."

"Click on it," Fenton had whispered.

Jonathan nodded, moved the cursor over the symbol, clicked, and the message opened.

Oh, forbidden dreams
Autumn feather-rain defense
Leather turtle's shell

"How the hell did she know about your e-mail?" had been the first words out of Jonathan's mouth.

And question #1 that Fenton carefully noted above his drawing of the computer. He pondered the note, then drew a circle around it. *If we can answer that question,* he thought, *then we will have the solution to the whole transfer question.*

But there had been more to come.

When they had recovered from their initial surprise, Fenton noticed that the scroll bar indicated there was more to the document, so Jonathan had scrolled down and the following line appeared:

Mono me ni mienai wa sora no ue ni desu.

"What the hell is that?" Fenton had asked.

Jonathan had leaned forward and studied the screen. "I don't believe this," he muttered. "It's Japanese. *In the sky above, invisible things,*" he translated. "The syntax is a little rough, but that's the gist of it."

"That doesn't make any sense."

Jonathan had slowly nodded his head. "Yes, it does. It's from the birth of the Buddha."

"I'll be damned," Fenton had exclaimed. "We've got a digital dragon lady."

The morning light etched the first soft traces of shadows across the wooded campground. The night rain had blown out sometime in the early hours of the morning, leaving an expectant sparkle on the still damp leaves and ground cover. A dawn breeze, hunting in the trees above the camper, shook loose droplets of water that tattooed briefly on the fiberglass roof over his head, refocusing his thoughts.

Fenton munched on the bagel, then picked up the ballpoint pen and wrote: Question #2- Is she Japanese? He drew another circle around both questions, then extended a connecting line down and drew a horizontal line. Beneath that he drew three shapes: a square, a triangle and a circle. He labeled these in sequence: when, where and how. From these he scribed three more lines that converged at the figure on the screen. More precisely, they converged on the question mark adorning the shapely figure. *If we can determine when a message arrived, and from where it originated, we would probably have the answer to how it was done. And, once we have the how,* he reasoned, *we are only a step away from the who.*

33

He felt a sudden flush of excitement he hadn't experienced since Mary Beth had peeled his hide in the judge's chambers. He sipped the coffee. *Damn,* he thought, *maybe Jonathan's right. Maybe this scraggly-assed old bulldog does have a few teeth left after all.*

CHAPTER 5

Naoko Matsuzawa stepped out of the rice-paper mist and joined the giggling crowd of Japanese schoolgirls squeezing onto the train at the Hase Station. Their blue and white uniforms and yellow backpacks created a colorful wave that swept her along as it flooded through the doors and down the aisle of the already crowded car. She managed to catch a pole between two blue-suited businessmen just as the doors closed and the electric locomotive jerked the coach into motion.

The rush hour train ride to Kamakura had been her morning routine for the past eighteen months, ever since she had moved back into the shadow of the Great Buddha. For her, the short commute was a never ending source of delight. The morning run was packed with commuters on their way to school and the shops and businesses in Kamakura, or to corporate offices further away in Yokohama and Tokyo. Later in the day the train would fill with expectant tourists or the faithful on their way to ponder the Great Buddha or pay homage at the Hasedera or Gokurakuji Temples. It was an intoxicating brew that she found endlessly fascinating.

She tightened her grip as the train started slowing for the Yugihama Station. She had even developed affection for the venerable cars and the rough roadbed of the Enoden Line. Compared to the modern JR Line, which continued north to Yokohama and Tokyo and south to Yokosuka and Kurihama, this ride was an adventure. The train rattled and jerked, and the cars pitched back and forth as it braked past the small station platform and finally screeched to a halt. She pressed against the pole as a few more businessmen and laughing students squeezed past, then the doors closed and they rumbled off again.

Minutes later Naoko was swept back off the train, along the platform and down the steps of Kamakura Station by the sea of suits and backpacks. Once in the station she worked herself out of the surging stream of commuters switching trains, and climbed the steps of the east exit just as the sun emerged from the mist like an unfolding fan. She paused as she stepped into its embrace and took a deep breath. A cool breeze hinting of autumn ruffled her dark hair and rustled the leaves in the nearby trees. It was as if the gods had reached down from their place in the heavens and cracked open the day just for her. She, like most of her friends, was not particularly religious in the traditional sense, but she had a finely tuned spirit that allowed her to see and hear small wonders that seemed to elude others. Her place in the universe had never been in question.

She listened to a leaf skate past, then took a deep breath of the sparkling air and crossed the street to the Burger King wedged tightly between two Japanese shops. Naoko loved American music, so she always stopped by this tiny outpost of the west to see what they were playing. Today it was Elvis Presley, so she bought a cup of tea and stood inside the door, trying to catch the English words. After one time through "Love Me Tender" she reluctantly pressed a cap on the Styrofoam cup, left the store and walked the few meters to the corner of Komachi-Dori Street. Here she paused again, trying to pick Elvis out of the street sounds, but her window on the west had closed, so she turned left, passed under a large, red Torii gate and headed for the gallery. *Perhaps,* she thought, *the kami-sama will smile today and send in an American so I can practice my English.*

Jonathan stared in disgust at the Facilities Brochure copy he had just retrieved from Stanley's desk. There were red notes written all over it, and entire paragraphs had been Xed out. *A few changes my ass,* he thought. He turned back to his desktop computer and read Stanley's inter-office e-mail again.

Jonathan, there are a few changes on the Facilities copy. Passed it by Hendrix before I left Friday, and he had some new ideas. As you will note, I've indicated his thoughts in the margins. I'll be out of town Tues. but will expect a rewrite on my desk Wed. AM. As you know, he needed it yesterday. Stanley

What a way to start the day, he thought.

"Problems?" a voice asked.

Jonathan looked up and saw Mildred standing beside his desk with an armload of files. "Oh. Hi, Mildred," he said, and held up the copy sheets. "Third rewrite in three days. Nobody seems to know what they want around here anymore."

She leaned forward. "Much less Stanley, right?" she asked.

Jonathan nodded. "Much less Stanley."

Mildred leaned further into his cubicle. "If you ask me, Jonathan, it sucks big time," she hissed.

Jonathan was taken totally by surprise. "Mildred, I've never heard you—"

"And, it's not just what they did to your copy, it's the whole damned place. It's going to hell in a hand basket." She paused long enough to catch her breath, then shifted the load of files, looked cautiously around and leaned back over his desk. "Just between you and me, I've got my resume out," she whispered through tight lips.

Jonathan gazed at her in disbelief. In the years they had worked together he had never known her to raise, or lower her voice in anger. "You really think it's that bad?" he asked tentatively.

"Jonathan, you're an intelligent, talented man. There's no future here. The merger is going to tear this company apart, and it's high time you figured that out."

With that, she reshifted her load and turned to leave, then stopped abruptly and stepped back close to his desk. "And, remember, you never heard me say a thing. I never said what you thought I said. After all," she smiled knowingly, "Mother Goose has an image to protect."

Jonathan stared at her departing figure. *Touché,* he thought. *The goose has turned.* He felt a sudden, newfound respect for this woman, and he was pleased that she had chosen him as her confidant and ally. *So much for my ability as a judge of character. I think Fent can definitely take her off the list,* he decided.

After Mildred left, Jonathan sat and pondered his ravaged copy. What had been, only a few minutes before, merely another frustrating example of management run amuck, now looked more like a corporate death certificate splashed with the red ink of his own blood. Jonathan tossed the offending pages on the desk. *Hell, maybe Mildred's right. Maybe the whole place is going down the tube.* He felt an immediate, chilling gust of apprehension. *Damn,* he thought. *The wolf may have finally found the door.* He sighed and looked at the clock. *Only 10:30,* he noted, *six hours until I see Margo.*

He leaned back in his chair, pictured the ancient Buddha, and listened for the voices of the spirits with his child's eye. As always, there was no reply, but the silence worked its magic and, after a few seconds, Jonathan breathed deeply, picked up his copy, and re-read Stanley's notes. *Okay, if that's what the Brothers Barbarossa want, that's what they'll get.* He reached for his phone and pressed an auto-dial button.

"Hi, Jennifer, it's me. How was your weekend?" He paused. "Happy to hear that. How does your afternoon look? We need to get together and go over the layout of the Facilities Brochure." He made notes on the copy while he spoke. "Two o'clock? Sure, that's great." He paused. "Yep, there've been more changes." He nodded and laughed. "Yeah, the barbarians are at the gate. See you at two."

Jonathan hung up the phone and glanced at the clock. *If I really get with it I can have a rough draft when I meet with Jennifer,* he thought. He scribbled a few more notes and turned to his desktop computer, then stopped and checked the clock again. He pondered the time, then pushed the copy sheets aside and bent down and unzipped the gym bag. He removed the laptop and placed it on the desk in front of him, then reached around the clock and carefully pulled a telephone cord up from behind the desk and plugged it into the side of the small computer. *Wonder if Fent's come up with anything,* he thought. But his mailbox was empty. *Guess it's too early for him to be at the café,* he reasoned. He was preparing to exit the program when a feminine voice suddenly announced: *"You have mail."* Jonathan felt his pulse quicken. He pressed the *Get Mail* button and the message appeared.

> *morning asshole,*
> *i assume this is a secure line. been doodling, which I've scanned and attached for ur amusement. if u have a minute check the "leather" file and see when it was created and where u and the computer were at that time. also, do u keep a journal or personal history on ur computer? if ur hooked up hit reply. i'll be here till 11:30. if i don't hear from u by then i'll check in later. keep it pointed into the wind.*
> *Manana*

Jonathan grinned, clicked the *Start* menu, then the *Explore* icon. The day was looking up.

Landon balanced the cell phone on his shoulder and spread mustard on a soy burger. When he was satisfied with his efforts he garnished it with bean sprouts and carefully capped off his creation with the top half of a sesame seed bun. A freshly scrubbed, pink-cheeked waitress in a bright green tee-shirt and white shorts placed a small bowl of fruit and a glass of carrot juice on the table just to the right of the burger. He studied the meal, then nodded his approval. It looked as if he had all the weapons in place for his daily battle with the renegade free radicals and toxic mutants rampaging through the guileless tissue of his body. The bright-eyed waitress hovered a second longer, then drifted on to her next table, accenting her retreat with a twitch of her tight little backside. The message was not lost on Landon, and he filed her tantalizing glances and teasing move in his "In" file for actress wannabes. Maybe next week—

The voice on the phone interrupted his rising fantasy. "Yes,

Peter." He nodded. "I'm still here." He pulled himself back into focus. "No, you're not interrupting anything, just another late lunch." He speared a huge strawberry. "Hang on a minute."

He slipped the strawberry into his mouth, then leaned over, opened his Gucci briefcase, removed a Palm Pilot computer and opened it on the table.

"Let me see, pardner." He punched the tiny keys and the screen lit up. "That's right, seven are on board plus you and me." He read the names as they scrolled up on the screen: "*John Langston, astral physicist; Lydia Brucker, photographer; Alan Breland, network finance; Sam Crantz, composer; Lorraine Bronson, director,* and the painter, *Topal Stein.*"

Landon paused and sipped the carrot juice. He watched the light filter through the greenery of the juice bar, and added another note to his cerebral shot list as the changing shadows on the tablecloth mamboed to the musical whir of the blender. He shifted the cell phone to the other ear and shook his head.

"Nothing from Jonathan since I spoke to him yesterday." He rotated the phone away from his chin and took a bite of the tofu burger.

"I expect to hear from him by the end of the week." Landon closed the little computer and slid it back into his case. "I agree, but he just needs a little time." He leaned forward on the table and his eyes narrowed. "Take my word for it, amigo, he's the right man. In fact, he's the only man. We can't do it without him."

The light bounced off Rodeo Drive turning the surrounding streets to sugar, and the blenders segued into a cinematic opening theme. Landon could see titles rolling, but he stayed totally focused on the conversation.

"I've shown you his work. We once did great stuff together, even you admit that, and dammit," Landon took a deep breath, "I don't have to remind you that the well is running dry. We're down to one show on the air, and we both agree that renewal is a toss-up." He paused, listening intently.

"That's past history. I think Jon can come back." His voice

tightened and he dug in. "Listen Peter, you leave the creative to me and I'll leave the business to you." Then the edge fell off his voice. "Besides, we have nothing to lose." He listened for a moment longer then visibly relaxed.

"That's great, compadre. One for all and all for one. I'll let you know as soon as I hear anything."

Landon snapped the phone off, laid it on the table, and sagged back into the chair. The last title scrolled past and the blenders ground to a stop. He let out a deep sigh.

He hated to admit it but, just as he had done in his agency days, he had ridden the creative horse so hard the exhausted beast was turning to mucilage. It had become the pattern of his life: get hot, go like hell, burn out; get back in the saddle, go like hell, burn out. It had always worked because of his enormous talent, but this time was different. This time he could feel the stumbling in his chest and could taste the ash of his fantasies in the smoke of his own fire.

In Atlanta he had gotten out of the agency with his star intact, before anybody realized what was going on and shipped him off to the glue factory. But L.A. was a different matter. He had been a power player, and during his meteoric rise he had left enough bruised egos in his dust to pave the Yellow Brick Road. There was already talk on the street, and Landon knew that here he could not pull off another last minute escape. If he were put out to pasture, it would be heralded in flashing lights all over the Hollywood Hills and nobody, but nobody, in the industry would give him a pot to piss in.

My only hope is that Jonathan can pull it off for me one more time, and, he thought, as he searched the restaurant, *the perky waitress with the white shorts and hot little body might like to make a down payment on becoming a star.*

CHAPTER 6

Fenton settled into the wire frame chair and set his coffee mug on the worn wrought iron table. The early afternoon sun played catch with the falling leaves and warmed the Harris Tweed. Its worn fibers sucked up the energy and insulated him against an early breath of fall sniffing around the potted shrubs that decorated the tiny courtyard of the Online Café. He stretched and yawned, then took a sip from the mug as he spread his notes out before him. He studied them for a minute, then shuffled their positions and pondered the resulting order again. He might just as well have been trying to read Tarot Cards for all the good it did him, he decided.

Once again, the mystery files had been created when Jonathan had the computer and was not connected to the Internet. The only other new information was that Jonathan did have a journal, his *Lotus Matrix* story synopsis, and some poems that Margo was having him write stashed away on his hard drive, but that was about it. Nothing to suggest who the Dragon Lady might be or what she was up to. *Except,* he thought, *she obviously knows a lot more about Jonathan than we know about her, which explains the Japanese stuff. But Jonathan had said her syntax was rough.* Fenton thumbed through the stack of paper until he came to his drawing of the computer and noted his written question: Is she Japanese?

It's not likely a native Japanese would stumble with grammar, he reasoned. He took a pen from the inside pocket of the Harris Tweed and started to doodle. After drawing several arrows at the question he stopped and underlined it; then he drew a vertical line down about an inch and wrote: Possibilities. Beneath that he listed: #1. Student of Japanese. #2. Knows a little Japanese, travels to Japan, not fluent. #3. Member of Japanese club, company, other organization. #4. All or none of the above.

He bundled his notes in a carefully drawn box, then added as an afterthought: Sakana Ya? He connected it to the box, then wrote: SatCom? And added it to the diagram. He considered his last two entries, then drew a question mark. There was no telling where else she might be, but one thing was obvious, the ball was in her court and, until she made a mistake or chose to step out of the shadows, she had them by the short hairs. *Which may not be all bad,* Fenton thought. *So far it's still a game and, if nothing else, she has our attention and has gotten my ass back in gear.*

He scooped up the papers, dumped them into a battered briefcase, picked up his mug and headed back into the café. It was time for his final Internet check before he hit the road. He nodded to Vincent as he stepped through the door and was pleased to see that R2D2 was available. He had developed a genuine fondness for the computer and had, on occasion, waited for over an hour when the machine was occupied. He wasn't sure what that meant, but he suspected it was a survival response of an ignored and undernourished libido. *Ah, well,* he thought, *at least the damn thing can't sue me.* He gave the monitor an affectionate pat, logged on and clicked the *You Have Mail* button when it popped up.

This is odd, he thought, when the screen appeared. He had one message from: *jnightingale. Subject: Oh, my!*

He read the name several times. "This must be a mistake. I don't know this person," he muttered. He read the subject line again, then shrugged and clicked on the *open* button.

"I'll be damned!" he blurted out when the message appeared:

Fantasy drawing
Two firm voluptuous mounds
Melting in your mouth

43

Naoko closed the glass door behind her and stood quietly in the hushed, early morning light of the gallery. It was her favorite moment of the day. The darkness was slipping away, stirring the spirits deep in the clay of the small pieces of sculpture and pottery slumbering on the pedestals, shelves and showcases in the room. She would not turn on the display lights until each object had awakened from the night and assumed the distinctive persona so carefully negotiated by its creator and the earth spirits. The recreation by the Nature Light was, to her, a sacred part of the creative process. It was the means by which she was formed each day and the birthright she bestowed on the art entrusted to her care.

The pieces near her, closer to the windows, were the first to assume their identities. Then, as the room continued to brighten, the cast of characters revealed themselves as if in a Kabuki play. When the smallest object in the farthest corner of the room realized its form, Naoko bowed to the assembled troupe, then stepped to the electrical panel behind the cash register counter and gently raised the lights.

After walking through the exhibition space to assure herself that each of her charges was in its proper place, she entered the gallery's small office, hung her coat on the back of the door and peeled the cap off her cup of tea. Yuki-*san* would be in later and the two of them would set up a small, enticing display on the sidewalk just outside the entrance, but until then she had the shop to herself. She settled into the desk chair, sipped her tea and pondered what was playing at the Burger King, then booted the computer on the desk before her.

While the machine warmed up she thumbed through the pile of receipts from the previous day. The sixth receipt was for a nine-inch clay figure and had a business card attached to it. She remembered the customer vividly. It was unusual for an American to speak Japanese fluently, especially an attractive, middle-aged woman. But what had most impressed Naoko was her gentle and kind manner. When Naoko had asked to speak in English the woman had obliged and, as they spoke, guided her English in a most gracious way. The thirty minutes they spent together had been the highlight of her day, and she wondered if she should thank Elvis Presley or the *kami-sama* for her good fortune.

Naoko unclipped the woman's card and studied the name. Mrs. David A. Livingson lived at House B, 1-13 Oppama Chu, Yokosuka, Japan. Following her address was her telephone number and e-mail address. The words were set in delicate black type on a white background.

It had been Mrs. Livingson's first time in the gallery, and she had wanted to be placed on the mailing list, so Naoko opened the computer's mail list program and carefully entered her name and address. After Naoko saved the entry, she picked up the card and read it again. Was it the rustle of fall leaves, or the plaintive melody of "Love Me Tender" whispering her name? She wasn't sure of the source of the subtle impulse, but it didn't matter. She always listened to her quiet voice and usually followed its counsel. Naoko considered the card one more time, then opened her small purse and slipped it inside.

Ten minutes later she finished filing the receipts and entering the other two mailing list requests just as the morning sun poked through the circular window high on the wall behind her. She glanced up as the rays of light traced across the wall and illuminated a small sculpture on the bookshelf facing her. *It must be about 8:30,* she thought. She looked at her watch. *Yuki-san will be in any minute; just time to check my e-mail.*

Naoko had her own computer, but Internet access was expensive, so for now Yuki allowed her to use the gallery computer and Internet service for her e-mail.

When the window opened there were seven messages waiting. She scanned the list. Six were for the gallery, but number three was for her. She leaned closer to the screen and read the announcement: *jnightingale. Subject: Ogenki desu ka.*

"Oh, it's Japanese Nightingale," Naoko exclaimed. She felt a ripple of excitement and double-clicked. The message appeared and she examined the text. After the greeting the next line was in English followed by its Japanese translation, then another line of English followed by its translation, and so it continued until the closing.

Sugoi! Her Japanese is improving, she thought. At that moment she heard the front door open.

"*Ohayo gozaimasu, Naoko-san,*" Yuki called out.

"*Ohayo gozaimasu, Yuki-san,*" Naoko replied.

I'll print this out and correct it later, she thought. "Talk to you soon Nightingale-*san*," she whispered, and closed the window.

CHAPTER 7

My life sap is seeping out;
a warm syrup tracing crimson and
pink roots in the snow.

How beautiful it is. How cleanly death
comes. Sharp and fresh, a clarion
call pure and clear, peeling down the mountain
splitting the wind, spinning my sac
into a silver chrysalis.

Margo finished reading the lines then looked over at the figure staring out the window. "How are you doing?" she asked.

"There's a lot going on," Jonathan answered.

"I agree, but I think we're getting somewhere."

Jonathan moved away from the window. "One step at a time, as they say." He smiled pensively and sat down on the sofa facing her. "You were right about putting it into words. It's like peeling an onion. I can't make up my mind whether to laugh or cry."

"You don't have to decide, you know. May I keep this? I'll add it to the first three verses."

Jonathan nodded. "Sure, it's on the computer."

"When you're finished I'd like to frame it. One for you and one for me."

"My graduation certificate?" he asked.

"More of a testament to courage," she replied.

"*Kachi wa saya no naka ni ari*. Victory comes while the sword is still in the scabbard."

Margo nodded. "Not bad, Grasshopper. *Iai-do,* correct?"

"You never cease to amaze me, Margo."

"I once had a few lessons with the sword."

Jonathan chuckled. "So that's where you learned your legendary discipline and self-control."

Margo's eye's flashed. "Ah, the secret to discipline is becoming the disciple. You should know that, Hopper."

Jonathan bowed slightly. "Duly noted, *sensei.*"

Margo returned the bow. "Shall we move along?"

"Abracadabra," Jonathan said.

Margo turned the page of her note pad. "How was the trip?" she asked.

Jonathan was silent for a moment. "All magic and mystery, like trying to catch lightning in a bottle. Landon still has the charisma to lead an army off a cliff."

"What are his marching orders?" Margo asked.

"He's putting together an eclectic group to come up with fresh programming ideas for prime time television."

Margo made a note on her pad. "Sounds interesting."

"That sort of thing *is* lightning in a bottle." Jonathan weighed the possibilities. "But, the question is, if he catches it what happens next? Will he be able to hold onto it?"

Margo caught his eyes. "How do you hold onto lightning, Jonathan?" she asked.

Jonathan pondered the idea. "That's very good."

Margo smiled.

Soft new age music filled the void while Jonathan considered the question. A long minute passed, then he leaned forward.

"When I was a child I would go out at night and catch lightning bugs. I would put them in a bottle, then I would take the glowing bottle in and put it beside my bed so I could have lightning in my room while I slept."

He paused and lingered over the memory. "Then the next

48

morning I would take the bottle out in the back yard and let the lightning bugs go."

Margo nodded. "Why did you do that?"

"So I could catch them again that evening."

Margo leaned toward him. They were almost touching. "Where was the magic, Grasshopper? In the catching or the keeping?" she whispered.

"In the catching," Jonathan replied.

Margo nodded. "Jonathan, whether you realize it or not, you're Landon's lightning. To keep it he must let it go."

She held his eyes for a second longer then sat back. "When do you have to make a decision?"

"I have to let him know something by the end of the week," Jonathan said.

"What about SatCom?"

"I've just started the annual report, so I couldn't leave for sixty days," he replied.

Margo floated on the incense and music, trying to catch the next wave. "That gives you some breathing room. Take your time with this, Jonathan. Listen to the music and dance *your* dance, not Landon's. Remember, you still have some onion left to peel and, while you're doing cosmic KP, just a reminder that tears and laughter come from the same place."

Jonathan slowly shook his head. "Margo," he said softly, "you're a hell of a woman."

Margo's eyes ignited and her red lips parted. "And don't you ever forget it, Jonathan."

She held the moment for another second, then picked up her notepad and turned to a new page. "Now, what about the Dragon Lady? Anything new since you called me?"

Jonathan sat back. "Not on my machine. But Fenton got an e-mail from her today."

Margo looked amused. "Hmm. Branching out. She certainly is a busy lady. What did she have to say?"

"Not much. Just commented on the drawing of her that Fent had e-mailed to me." He smiled. "It was another haiku and, tongue-in-cheek you might say."

"Showing off a little, and keeping you boys in a sweat. I like her sense of humor." She thumbed through the notepad. "I've checked with some hacker friends and they're impressed. None of them can figure out how she's doing it. I've also made a little trip to the stars, and I haven't picked up any negative energy."

"Then it's an elaborate joke?"

"It's possible, but I doubt it. These things can be complicated. Just because I didn't pick up any bad vibes doesn't mean they're not there. She's obviously very clever at concealing herself, so I may have surfed right past her. And, this is taking a lot of effort on her part. For whatever reason, she's really into it."

"As in obsession?" Jonathan asked.

Margo made a note in her pad. "I don't know, it's too soon to tell. One thing for sure, right now it's her dance and, for the moment, she's holding the card with your name on it. What's her e-mail ID?"

"Jnightingale," Jonathan replied.

Margo wrote it down. "Interesting," she observed. "Yours is jlseagull."

"Both are birds. Birds of a feather—"

"Flock together," Margo finished the sentence. "It may be only a coincidence, but still, I wonder what the J stands for?"

"Maybe *joke*, as in 'the joke's on you'."

Only the briefest hint of a smile teased her face. "Maybe it is. Can you track her by her e-mail address?"

"Fent's working on that." He looked at his watch. "In fact, I'm meeting him in twenty minutes."

Margo closed her notepad. "Then it's a good time to wind up this session." She reached out and took his hands and closed her eyes. They sat that way for a few seconds while she aligned their energy; then she released him and they stood up. Jonathan pulled on his jacket while Margo walked over to the breakfront and picked up her appointment book.

"See you for dinner Thursday."

Jonathan was at the door. "That's right. I'm looking forward to it."

Margo was still looking at her calendar. "And thank you for referring Jennifer Mitford; she's a very interesting person."

"Jennifer Mitford?" Jonathan stopped with his hand on the doorknob. "I don't remember referring Jennifer."

"I'm pretty sure that's what she said. She used your name when she called for her appointment."

He stood holding the knob. "I may have mentioned you at lunch last week. I'm your one-man PR firm, you know." He shook his head. "But I've really been out of it lately. Anyway, she's a neat person. See you Thursday." He turned the knob and went out.

But Margo didn't reply, and she never heard the door close. She was standing perfectly still, transfixed. The psychic wind had come back up, and she was listening intently to what sounded like leaves skating on a distant street.

Jennifer turned off the headlights, took the key out of the ignition, and sat perfectly still in the seat of the red Miata. She carefully searched the parking lot of the Old Carriage Factory and noted that most of the parking spaces were filled. She was thankful that when the building was converted to lofts, the developers had ringed the parking area and perimeter of the property with an abundance of period street lamps. Not only did they complement the architecture of the old building, but their warm glow created an island of security within the gated community. Security had been one of the main features that attracted her to the Factory and made it possible to overcome her natural caution and move into the transitional, industrial area. She knew the system wasn't bulletproof, but it certainly seemed up to the task, and she had felt comfortable until the last three weeks.

Once she was satisfied that the parking lot presented no danger, she studied the approach to her front door. Most of the condo entrances were off hallways inside the building, but hers was one of a few that opened to the outside onto the parking area. In the original factory it had been the entrance to the shipping department. Jennifer had chosen it because it was a corner unit and she liked its convenience and privacy. A bonus was the walled area off the back that allowed for a small patio and space for her to garden.

From where she sat everything looked in order. The street lamp at the corner of the building illuminated the walkway that led to her unit, and the entrance light to the right of her door was on. She looked at her watch. In five minutes Harold Gonzales, the security guard, would be making his rounds in his golf cart. From all outward appearances it was just another peaceful evening at the Old Carriage Factory. She checked the parking area again, slung her purse and computer bag over her shoulder, got out and headed for her apartment, front door key in hand.

Jennifer never saw the shadow separate from the Chevrolet Impala parked two cars down and slip up behind her. She didn't sense danger until the front door was unlocked, and then it was too late. Her head hit the door frame and the breath was knocked out of her as she was pushed, sprawling into the front hall.

Jonathan squeezed between two wrought iron benches, stepped out onto the sidewalk and was nearly bowled over by a huge Doberman leading a blonde runner at the end of a red leash. The lady in spandex smiled and never slowed as he attempted to hang on to his gym bag while stumbling against the benches. When he regained his balance and looked up, the two had rounded the corner and were out of sight. *Damn, this is a dangerous neighborhood,* he thought. He looked both ways, then stepped cautiously across the walkway and reached for the door knob of the Online Café.

"You realize you're the only person other than my priest who knows about this place, don't you?" Fenton asked, when Jonathan had settled into the soda fountain chair at the small table.

"I didn't know you had a priest."

"Safety net. I did it for my mother. Somebody had to know where to start looking in case anything happened to me. God knows I've given her enough grief, so it was the least I could do. Besides, it never hurts to cover all the bases."

Jonathan nodded. "You've got a point."

Fenton sat back. "Your California Club and espresso will be up in a minute."

"Thanks. If I live to eat it. I was damn near run over on the way in here by a—"

The freckles around Fenton's eyes danced. "That was Frieda and Heinrich. Every morning and every evening like clock-work they wear a path around the block. The locals know the schedule and tread with caution." He squinted at his watch. "They'll make their last pass of the day in twelve minutes, give or take thirty seconds."

"That's amazing."

"A knockwurst and California club?" The kid with green hair had materialized beside their table with two sandwich baskets.

Fenton looked up. "That's us."

The boy put the baskets on the table. "And one espresso?"

"That's right."

"Can I get you anything else?" the boy asked.

"I think we're in good shape, Skywalker," Fenton answered.

"I'll be on the Death Star if you need me, Junkdog." He turned away and headed for the wall of computers.

"Skywalker?" Jonathan watched the boy hitch up his chair in front of a computer.

"That's his Internet ID. All the regulars go by their IDs in here."

Jonathan unwrapped his sandwich. "And you're Junkdog."

Fenton inspected the knockwurst and added a little salt and pepper. "That's me."

"So nobody in here knows your real name."

"Only Vincent." He nodded toward the figure at the cash register. "In case the priest calls."

"No wonder you like this place."

"It's every man's dream." Fenton stirred his coffee. "How's Margo?"

"She's on all four burners. Any luck tracking the Dragon Lady's e-mail address?"

Fenton pushed the sandwich to one side, reached under the table and pulled his notes from his battered brief case. "Dead end unless she threatens you or commits a crime of some sort. The Internet providers can't and won't reveal their customers identities without a court order, and we would have to show a pretty serious threat exists to get a judge to go along with that." He laid the papers beside his basket. "What's Margo's take on the Dragon Lady?"

"Right now I think she's amused by the whole thing. So far she hasn't picked up any malevolent energy, but she didn't rule it out, so only time will tell. She's going to make periodic passes through the galaxy and she'll keep me informed."

"Uh huh." Fenton's face wrinkled in disbelief.

"She was also interested that both our e-mail ID's are birds."

Fenton nodded. "That *is* of interest." He pulled out his pen and made a note. "Did she—"

He was interrupted by a muffled musical sound.

Jonathan held up his hand. "Hold that thought." He reached down and unzipped the gym bag and took out a cell phone. He studied the readout for a second then punched the receive button. "Hi Jennifer. What's going—"

The voice on the line broke in. "Jonathan—" Then she hesitated, as if trying to decide what to say next. "I really hate to bother you." He immediately felt fatigue and anxiety squeezing her words. "But, I need to talk to somebody."

"What's wrong, Jennifer?" he asked.

"I hope this is all right, but I tried you at home and there was no answer."

"It's all right. I'm having dinner with a friend. What's going on?"

"I don't want to talk on the phone." Fear crept in among the tendrils of stress.

"Where are you?"

"At home."

"The Carriage Factory?"

"Yes, 5A." Then, as an afterthought, "It's on the corner of the building."

"I'll be right there."

"No, finish your dinner. I'm okay."

But from the sound of her voice, he wasn't so sure. He looked at his watch. "Jennifer, I'm leaving now. I'll be there in twenty minutes."

He sensed her relief. "I'll notify security at the gate that you're coming."

"See you in a few minutes."

"Thank you, Jonathan." The connection parted and she was gone.

Jonathan pressed the phone off and stared at the handset. He had an undefined feeling of foreboding.

"A lady in distress?" Fenton asked.

Jonathan looked up. "Something's really upset Jennifer. I'm going to have to go. Sorry about dinner."

"Understood. Does she do this often?"

"No." Jonathan zipped the gym bag, pushed back from the table and stood up. "As a matter of fact she's never called me outside of work before."

"Must be pretty—" Fenton frowned and squinted through the window into the gathering darkness. "This is odd." He checked his watch. "Frieda and Heinrich are three minutes overdue."

CHAPTER 8

It had been a quiet day at the gallery. After checking their e-mail, Naoko and Yuki arranged the teaser display on a table to the right of the gallery's entrance. The space was ideal for the purpose since the front door was sheltered and set back from the sidewalk at an angle, allowing space for potential customers to stop and examine the artful objects at their leisure.

The display had proved very successful in attracting customers inside. Naoko was especially pleased, because taking the art outside to draw people into the gallery had been her idea. She had approached Yuki with her plan several months after she started work.

Naoko initiated the conversation by commenting on the lovely space around the entrance, and that she had noticed how passers-by enjoyed pausing in its shelter to peer through the window at the current exhibition. Then she noted the busy pace of life along the street, and how people who had stopped usually hurried quickly on their way. Naoko then let the subject drop.

Since Maeda Yuki was her employer and several years her elder, Naoko was careful to maintain a proper level of respect and not approach her too directly with requests and ideas. Of course she had always referred to her politely as Maeda-*san*.

Then a few days later, when they were standing in the door of the gallery, Naoko brought up her idea again. "It is quite refreshing out today," she observed. "It is so nice to enjoy art outside, don't you think, Maeda-*san*?" she asked.

Maeda considered the thought then smiled. "The Rolling Stones are playing at the Burger King today, Matsuzawa-*san*. Let's close the gallery for a few minutes and walk down and get some tea."

Naoko was stunned. Before she could answer, Maeda locked the door and they were threading their way along the gray and white tiles of the crowded street.

"You seem surprised that I would like western music," Maeda said. They stepped aside for a delivery truck inching its way slowly through the congested foot traffic.

Before Naoko could find words to answer, she continued. "You see, Matsuzawa-*san*, I lived with my cousin in California for two years and, while I was there, I studied art history at the University of Southern California. I returned to Kamakura because this is my home and my family is here, but when I came back I brought some American ways and ideas with me."

"I don't know what to say, Maeda-*san*," was all Naoko could manage to utter. The idea of living in California had taken her breath away.

Maeda turned to her. "I understand your feelings, Matsuzawa-*san*. That is one of the reasons I employed you." She paused and smiled. "When you find your voice, you may speak to me of any ideas or wishes you may have. I think I know what you have been trying to say the past few days, but it does not have to be my idea. I want to hear it from you."

"Thank you, Maeda-*san*." Naoko bowed slightly.

Maeda acknowledged the bow. "And, if we're going to listen to the Rolling Stones together, I prefer that you address me as Yuki-*san*. I consider us to be friends."

That brief conversation on the way to the Burger King had been an epiphany for Naoko. She felt honored by Maeda's acceptance of her, and she resolved to do everything she could to be worthy of her friendship. She also determined to be open to any unexpected wonders from the west stirring on the east wind.

She was standing in the entrance thinking of that day, now over a year ago, when she heard the phone ring in the office. A moment later Yuki stepped into the gallery and called excitedly to her.

"Naoko-*san* you have a call. It's from a Livingson-*san* and she wants to place an order."

Naoko was taken totally by surprise. "She wants to talk to me?" she asked.

"Yes. She asked to speak to you."

"Oh, my." Naoko hurried into the office.

"I think it's the American woman who was in the other day. Her Japanese is excellent," Yuki whispered, as Naoko picked up the phone.

Naoko took a breath and composed herself. "*Moshi, moshi. Matsuzawa desu,*" she said in her most bell-like voice.

"*Moshi, moshi, Matsuzawa-san. Elizabeth Livingson desu,*" the voice on the line answered. "Would you like to speak English?"

"*Hai.* Yes. I would like to speak English, Livingson-*san.*" She felt herself begin to relax.

Yuki gave her a thumbs-up gesture.

Naoko put her hand to her face, then smiled and sat down in the desk chair.

"I am so happy you are in today, Matsuzawa-*san.* I enjoyed our conversation when I was in the gallery."

"I, too, am pleased, Livingson-*san.*" Naoko was so excited she hoped she wouldn't stumble over words and make a fool of herself. "How may I be of help?"

"I would like to order another figurine like the one I bought yesterday. I hope you have one left."

Naoko's mind flashed through her English-Japanese dictionary. Figurine was a new word, but the Japanese word for figure was *zu,* and yes, Livingson-*san* had purchased a *nendo no zu,* a figure of clay.

"Yes, we have two figu-rines left," she said carefully.

"Oh, I am very pleased." Livingson-*san* sounded genuinely delighted. "Would it be possible for you to save one for me? I will be in Kamakura tomorrow, and I will pick it up."

"I would be happy to do that, Livingson-*san.*" Naoko made a note on a pad by the phone.

"I will be there around eleven-thirty." Mrs. Livingston paused. "Would you have lunch with me?"

Naoko felt a shiver of expectation. "I would be honored, Livingson-*san*," she replied.

"Then I will see you about eleven-thirty. *Mata ashita*, see you tomorrow, Matsuzawa-*san*.

"Yes, *mata ashita*, Livingson-*san*," Naoko said and slowly placed the handset in its cradle just as a gentle breeze from the open door rustled the papers on the desk.

The wrought iron gate guarding the entrance to the Old Carriage Factory closed behind Jonathan as he rolled slowly forward and studied the parking area. The guard had directed him to the right, toward the end of the large sprawling building, where he could see the front door light and the illuminated windows of unit five. A red Miata was parked just to the left of the walkway. *That's her car, so this must be the place,* he decided. He parked in the next space, got out of the car and started up the walk. The warm streetlights and the restoration ambiance did nothing to dispel the uneasy feeling that had accompanied him since Jennifer's phone call. He took a deep breath and reached for the doorbell.

Margo had been immediately attracted to the handsome woman seated at the table across from her in the bookstore café. She estimated her age at anywhere from the middle fifties to early sixties, but she reminded herself, looks can be deceiving. One thing was certain, she radiated an aura of quiet strength that Margo sensed came from a life well lived.

But what had really caught Margo's eye was her choice of reading material. After the woman had unwrapped her muffin and uncapped her cup of tea, she had opened a small volume on Japanese verbs. She thumbed through its pages while tasting the muffin and sipping her tea, stopping occasionally to study an entry.

Interesting, Margo thought. *Reading Japanese grammar is not something most people do for pleasure.* She took her last sip of papaya juice and a final bite of salad. *She must be a student,* she decided, but before she could speculate further, the woman closed the book and prepared to leave. On an impulse, Margo quickly stood up and followed her as she headed for the checkout counter.

In line at the cashier's, Margo stood as close to the woman as she dared; close enough to catch a whiff of her perfume. The fragrance of Shalimar was barely detectable. Shalimar was Margo's favorite fragrance. *She has good taste,* she thought. When her turn came to pay, the woman laid two books on the counter. Margo felt a sudden, electric tingle. The second book was titled *The Complete Guide to Computer Operating Systems. Who is this?* she wondered.

The sales clerk rang up the purchase. "That will be thirty-seven-fifty," she announced.

The woman reached into her purse and took out her wallet. Margo leaned slightly forward and to her right hoping to see the name on her credit card, but she was disappointed. The woman paid the exact amount in cash, thanked the clerk, took the bag with her books and turned to leave.

Margo caught a final tease of Shalimar as she stepped to the counter. She paid quickly for her meal and the magazine she had purchased, then hurried to the door and out into the parking lot. But she was too late. The woman was nowhere in sight, and it was impossible in the dark to tell which car slipping in and out of traffic might be hers. She took a deep breath, stood quietly and closed her eyes. The surf was up, but now the cosmic breeze carried on its wings a definable hint of Shalimar.

Two hours later Jonathan was back at his apartment seated in front of his laptop computer. He pressed the power button and, while the machine whirred to life, reached down and scooped Hemingway up from his usual place curled beside Jonathan's chair. Once in his lap, Hemingway rolled over and Jonathan slowly scratched his ears and chest. Almost immediately he felt rhythmic purring beneath his fingers. It was a comforting sensation.

When the desktop screen settled down, Jonathan clicked on *E-*

Mail, then *Address Book*, then Fenton's address. He exhaled slowly and replayed the events of the past two hours, then he leaned forward and started to write.

Fent,
We have a lady in distress. Jennifer has a very serious problem. She had a break-in tonight and she needs an attorney, and not just any attorney, but a real, take-no-prisoners bulldog like yourself. Don't want to email details so call me as soon as you get this and you and I can meet. If you pick this up tomorrow call at work. I'll hold lunch open. Fent, the lady needs help.
Ja mata. AEKDB

Jonathan clicked *Send* and watched as the screen flashed *Mail Sent.* Then he sat back, let out a sigh, reached through time for the Buddha and stroked Hemingway.

It seemed only a second later, or perhaps he had dozed off, when the phone rang. He jumped, dislodging Hemingway, and reached for the receiver. "Hello."

"So, the lady has a serious problem," the familiar voice on the line said.

"Fent. Didn't think you would still be at the café." He leaned down and consoled Hemingway.

"I was just closing down when you came through. You can surf only so much sex before it all starts to look the same, as you probably know."

"You're really bad. One of these days—"

"Yeah, I know."

Jonathan could hear him sipping a drink.

"So, Jennifer is in some kind of trouble?"

"An intruder forced his way into her apartment tonight."

"Robbery?"

"That wasn't what he was after."

"Oh, shit."

"She's okay, only a little bruised. He left when she threatened to call security."

"Can she identify him?"

"She knows him."

"She knows him?"

"Yeah."

"Did she report it?"

"She can't."

"Why not?"

"Not on the phone. Are you interested?"

There was silence on the other end of the line, and Jonathan knew Fenton was working through a lot of history. Finally, he heard the sipping sound; then Fenton answered.

"What time?"

A weight lifted off Jonathan. "It's your call. I have some stuff due in the morning, but Jennifer can cover if I'm out."

"How about noon at the café. We can sit outside where nobody will bother us."

"When do you want to meet with Jennifer?"

"You and I need to talk first. Remember, it's been a while."

"I'll be there at noon."

"By the way, I got the old fraternity handshake at the end of your e-mail. That was nasty, brother."

"I thought you'd like that."

"Uh-huh. You owe me one." There was the sipping sound, then Fenton hung up.

Jonathan replaced the phone and turned to the computer. The e-mail program was still up so he clicked out of it. The desktop came up, and he was preparing to turn the machine off when his eye was drawn to the display of icons. He leaned forward and stared at the screen. There, right next to *My Documents* was a new file titled *Once Wounded*.

Jonathan exhaled slowly, then double-clicked on the icon and the document opened.

A bitter east wind
The once wounded crane beset
Cannot find his way

The words were carefully centered in the middle of the page. Jonathan read and reread the message and then leaned wearily on the table and turned the machine off.

CHAPTER 9

The traffic light faded from red to green, but nothing moved—Wilshire Boulevard was a lock. Landon groaned, set the hand brake and adjusted the volume on the CD player. Vivaldi erupted from the silver Porsche, transforming the morning "ode to noxious hydrocarbons" into "The Rites of Spring."

A Paleolithic, sun-dried blonde in a red Rolls in the next lane eyed him through her Foster Grants, then closed the magazine she was reading and tapped her driver on the shoulder. He reached for something on the door, her window rolled down and she flashed Landon a blinding set of matched dentures. He nodded, and immediately regretted the impulse.

Encouraged, she leaned forward and mouthed, "What are you doing tonight, daahling?"

Landon flinched, then held up his left hand and pointed to the gold band on his ring finger. She puckered frosted lips, mouthed "too bad" and tapped the driver again. The window rolled up, and she went back to living out her fantasies in the pages of Cosmo.

Landon did a rapid replay, but this time the blonde was Sharon Stone, he was Nick Cage and she was driving a yellow Lamborghini. And, instead of mouthing the invitation, Sharon would recognize him, check Internet Celebrity Search and call on his cell phone. It was a much more satisfying scenario.

The scene played out as the light ran through its sequence again and the Rolls inched forward. Landon pulled focus back to the traffic jam and did a quick cut to the perky waitress at the juice bar. Too bad that wasn't her in the Rolls. Then he would create a different ending for this little melodrama. *Oh, well, maybe it's not too late,* he thought, *maybe at lunch.*

From behind him Landon heard sirens and could see blue and red lights filling his rear-view mirror. *Goddamn, I hate that sound,* he thought. He flinched as a wailing ambulance squeezed past followed by an LAPD black-and-white. Vivaldi had met his match, so Landon punched the player off and discovered his cell phone was ringing. A tight close-up of Sharon Stone fingering a tiny keypad flashed on his screen. He caught his breath and glanced at the back of the aging blond. There was no cell phone in sight and she appeared lost in her reading. *Thank God,* he thought and pressed the recieve button.

"Landon here," he said, cupping his hand around the handset as the sirens faded in the distance.

"Peter. Yeah, I know. I'm stuck on Wilshire. Accident of some kind has everything backed up." He released the hand brake and the Porsche inched forward three feet. The blond put down the magazine, looked over and smiled as if she were warming up for another run on him.

Landon frowned. "Nishikawa called?" A horn honked behind him. A cop was pointing and waving him through the intersection.

"He's flying in from Tokyo? What the hell's going on?" His stomach tightened and he grimaced as the blonde held up a cell phone. Traffic was starting to move.

"Peter, I don't like the sound of this." He moved the phone to his left hand so he could shift with his right. The blonde was falling back.

"Yeah, but he wouldn't be unless Takamoto—" He paused, listening intently. The Rolls was closing in again.

"And that was it? He's just dropping by to touch base." Landon eased to the left to avoid a patch of shattered glass on the road and the emergency vehicles surrounding the accident site. The palms of his hands were damp.

"Of course I don't believe it; Takamoto's bean counters have been crunching the numbers." He maneuvered around the last EMS.

"Calm down, amigo, we've got three days. Circle the wagons and call a meeting for this afternoon, and Peter, keep it to yourself. We don't want this on the street." The traffic behind Landon came to a halt while a wrecker maneuvered into position to remove a crumpled Isuzu.

Landon ground second gear and gritted his teeth. "For God's sake, Peter, take a pill and lie down. I should be there in five minutes."

He snapped off the phone and wiped his hands dry on his trousers while checking his rearview mirror. The predatory Rolls was still blocked by the wrecker. He was suddenly overcome by the forlorn desperation of the blonde. *We're both fucking has-beens,* he thought, *a day late, a dollar short, and shit-out-of-luck.*

Jonathan picked a corner table close to a potted shrub and as far away from the door as possible. He ducked under the sheltering maroon umbrella, and after carefully setting his coffee mug, Danish and briefcase on the decorative wrought iron next to the salt and pepper shakers, he gently settled his complaining body into a chair. He had arrived early and was thankful that, except for a ladybug exploring the napkin holder and a butterfly looking for a fix, he had the café courtyard to himself. He checked his watch. Fenton wouldn't be there for another thirty or forty minutes, which gave him much needed time to organize his thoughts and sort through the load of stuff Landon had e-mailed him overnight.

The events of the previous evening and the appearance of the Dragon Lady's latest message had taken their toll, and he had slept fitfully. He finally went belly up for good around five o'clock. If it hadn't been for Hemingway leaping on him demanding breakfast, he would probably still be out. *But at least I didn't have the dream,* he thought. That would have been unbearable. He had come to the conclusion his psyche must be fused to selectively break pain circuits when the load threatened to be too great; how else to explain the fact that he hadn't shorted out and blown a fuse, or worse, by now? Everyday somebody lost it and jumped out of a building or shot up their broker's office, yet somehow he always managed to survive, and usually with at least a shred of his humanity and humor intact. On this morning that was good enough.

Jonathan finished the Danish and set the coffee mug down. The caffeine and sugar were doing their job and his head was beginning to clear. *Okay,* he thought, *time to suck it up and get in gear.* He sat perfectly still, took a slow, deep breath in and out, then unzipped his case and removed a manila folder.

The first couple of pages were notes from the Monday night Abracadabra session. From the list of names it appeared that everyone on the team was present. Several story concepts had been presented followed by lively debate. It was clear from Landon's memo that this was a challenging and enthusiastic group. Jonathan felt a tentative nudge of adrenalin as he thumbed through synopses of the three concepts they had chosen for further consideration. At the next meeting any new ideas would be added to those three. At the end of the session a vote would be taken and those concepts considered promising would be left in the pot. Landon hoped to have three ideas ready for development in four weeks.

Maybe he is on to something, Jonathan thought. He pushed the night fog to one side and scanned the three proposals again. Not bad. He could see definite possibilities for numbers one and three. Landon wanted him to grade them on a scale from one to five, so he marked them accordingly then closed the folder. *The sly old bastard is trying to set the hook,* he thought, as he slid the file back into the case.

The ladybug came to the edge of the napkin holder and froze, apparently perplexed by the abyss ahead of her. Jonathan pondered her options, then pushed the briefcase aside and leaned down as close to her as he could.

"It's not the edge of the world. Go for it," he whispered.

She lingered for another millisecond, as if screwing up her courage, and then stepped off into space.

"So, now he's talking to bugs."

Jonathan looked up in surprise.

Fenton grinned over the napkin holder.

"How long have you been here?" Jonathan was dumbfounded.

"Long enough."

"God, I never saw you sit down."

"You were talking to a bug, bro."

"Caught me red-handed."

Fenton shook his head. "Uh-huh."

Jonathan shrugged. "What can I say?"

"How about, I need help."

"I'd say the old bulldog is feisty today. You sleep with a snake last night?"

"Just trying to get in shape for business. As I said, it's been a while." Fenton hesitated and asked the question with his eyes before he said it. "How am I doing?"

"You fooled me, Counselor."

Fenton seemed satisfied. "Okay." He reached for his worn briefcase. "Let's talk about Jennifer."

Jonathan felt a sucking sensation as the energy drained out of him. It was as if the morning were starting over again and Hemingway had just dragged him from bed. He attempted to find his way back through the dark hedgerows and refocus his thoughts. Once he had found his place he sat back, reached for reverse gear and shifted to the night before. When he arrived at the scene and the players were in position, he took a deep breath and leaned forward.

"Get out your legal pad, Fent. You're not going to believe this."

"When did the abuse begin?" Margo asked gently.

Jennifer turned away. The subdued light limned her face with melancholy tones. For a brief instant Margo feared she might lose her; that the demons of those years might yet blot out her soul. But after what seemed an eternity, the threatening umber dissolved and she, as if by an act of primal courage, slowly emerged from the shadows.

"Eighteen months after my father died, my mother remarried." Jennifer paused as she worked her way back through the years.

"David Finley had an MBA and a job with a large corporation, and mother had been having a hard time making ends meet."

She spoke softly and tentatively. Margo had to listen carefully to catch her words.

"There hadn't been any other men in her life, and the offer of financial security plus the attention, and he was very handsome...." Her eyes misted. "I think he kind of swept her off her feet."

"How did you feel about a new man in your mother's life?" Margo asked.

Jennifer turned slowly back to her. "It was wonderful to see my mother happy again."

"How about you?"

"He was very attentive. He brought me presents and played with me and made me laugh." She smiled sadly. "I was happy, too."

For a fleeting moment, Margo saw a golden child seated before her and heard the laughter in her eyes. Then as quickly as she had appeared, the little girl retreated into the shadows and the woman re-emerged.

"Then we moved into a big new house, and two days later David took me onto his lap for the first time."

Jennifer brushed her eyes with the back of her fingers. Margo removed a tissue from a box on the table beside them and passed it to her.

"I know this is painful. We can stop for today if you would like."

Jennifer patted her eyes with the tissue. "Thank you." She attempted a faint smile. "I think I'm okay."

"We're not on a time schedule, so if at any time you would like to take a break."

Jennifer nodded. "You're very kind."

Margo paused to organize her thoughts. "How old were you the first time?"

"It was on my mother's birthday. I was seven years old." Margo noticed Jennifer's shoulders had relaxed slightly, but her hands were clasped tightly in her lap clutching the tissue.

"And how long did it go on?"

"Until Mother divorced him. I was fourteen."

"After the divorce, did you ever see him again?"

Jennifer's hands turned to knots. "Not until three weeks ago when he suddenly appeared at my door."

"He appeared at your door?" Margo asked in disbelief.

Jennifer nodded numbly, and a dark wash of fear fell across her face.

"He tried to pick up where he had left off."

Dear Japanese Nightingale-san,

I have the gallery to myself this morning. Yuki-san is visiting her mother and the day is early, so I think to send you email.

Naoko sipped her tea as the morning sun found an opening in the clouds and brightened the small office.

I had dinner last night with father. We ate at very nice restaurant in Yokohama where he has office. Since he took over company from his father and I moved to Kamakura we do not see as much of each other. Company is huge and he is very busy. He and my mother worry that I am not married, but he is very proud of my job and understands new ways of young people. He asked about you and sends best wishes, kokoro wo komete—from his heart.

I must tell you of a new American friend. She is customer of the gallery. Her name is Mrs. David Livingson and she lives in Yokosuka. She came in and bought a figurine and we hit it off as you say. Her Japanese is totemo joozu desu, so good if I closed my eyes I think she is from Tokyo. I am very excited, because today we are going to have lunch. I think she has much to tell me about America and I can show her much new of Japan.

I still plan to visit you next summer. My father wants me to travel sooner, but Yuki-san gives me more responsibility and gallery business is growing so I should not leave until then. The sun is over statue so it's time to say goodbye. Write soon.

Naoko

Naoko took a final sip of tea, then moved the curser to the *Send* button. She was preparing to click when the telephone rang. She hesitated then reached for the handset.

"*Moshi, moshi. Shiki Gallery. Matsuzawa Naoko desu.*"

"*Moshi, moshi, Matsuzawa-san.* This is Mrs. Livingson. I am so happy you answered."

Naoko was immediately aware of an undercurrent of stress in Mrs. Livingson's voice. "Thank you Livingson-*san.* Yes, it's me. How may I help you?"

"I am so sorry Naoko-*san,* but I will have to cancel lunch today. There is a family emergency," she said with a mix of urgency and regret.

Naoko felt her heart open with Mrs. Livingson's spontaneous use of her given name and the sound of distress in her voice.

"Oh, Livingson-*san,* I am sorry for emergency. Lunch is okay. May I be of help?"

"*Goshinsetsu ni,* you are very kind, Naoko-*san.* I am at a hospital, but please don't worry. I will call you soon so we can have lunch."

"I look forward to lunch, Livingson-*san,* but please take care. I will think of you."

"Thank you, Naoko-*san.*"

After Mrs. Livingson hung up, Naoko watched the sunlight explore the sculpture on the bookcase and tried to compose her thoughts. Livingson-*san* was obviously in distress and Naoko wished she could be of help. Naoko remembered she was calling from a hospital. It would be difficult to be a foreigner in a Japanese hospital. *Perhaps father can help,* she thought. *He has great power and can arrange anything. He will be able to find Livingson-san, and if there are problems he will smooth them out and make sure the family receives the very best care.*

The sunlight had moved past the bookcase and was wandering along the wall. Naoko turned back to the computer and scrolled to the bottom of her letter.

One more message Nightingale-san: I am distressed. Livingson-san just called on telephone and we are not having lunch. There is emergency in her family and she was at hospital. I worry for her and family health. Maybe Father can help.

Naoko clicked on *Send* then picked up the phone and dialed. The number rang three times then a friendly female voice answered.

"*Moshi, moshi.* Takamoto International. Takamoto Takeo's office. This is Tomita Chino."

"*Moshi, moshi,* Tomita-*san.* Is Father in?"

David Finley was annoyed. He checked his hand-held computer for the fourth time. The Ferret was thirty minutes overdue for his scheduled check-in. He laid the device on the car seat beside him, studied his fingernails and his mood darkened. He had broken the nails on his left index finger and thumb when he shoved Jennifer through the door of her apartment. Their ragged edges contrasted sharply with the others' perfect symmetry, setting off a visceral pulsing in his jaw.

Goddamn it, I shouldn't have pushed her so hard, he thought, *but she has to learn, and at least I got inside before that damned security guard showed up.* David picked up the computer and glared at the screen. Still nothing. He checked his watch. *It's 2 a.m. in Tokyo,* he calculated. *It would be just like that idiot to forget to set his alarm clock. I can't sit here in the parking lot much longer; people will begin to miss me. I'll give him five minutes,* he fumed.

David took a nail file and buffer from his suit coat pocket and began to carefully shape the offending nails. When he was satisfied he buffed and polished one and then the other. His fingers were slender and sensitive, a source of pride and instruments of his obsessions, and he took great pleasure in the physical gratification they provided him. He massaged his palms and his mind drifted to Jennifer. Her resistance only added to his anticipation. The twitch in his chin was replaced by a warm rush spreading up through his body.

He reached for a men's magazine open to a center spread on the seat beside him, but his fantasy was abruptly terminated by a sudden buzzing from the computer.

His mood instantly changed. *At last.* He clicked on the highlighted mail icon and the message opened. He quickly scanned the three lines on the screen. *Excellent,* he thought, *we're getting close.* Then he frowned.

"More money?" he said aloud. *Damn, will it ever stop? But, we're almost there,* he reminded himself. He ground his teeth and hit *Reply.*

Excellent work. Time is of the essence. Check account after 12PM.

He signed off, unclipped a cell phone from his belt and dialed.

"Stanley, the client requires additional billing." He frowned, listening intently.

"I know the budget's tight, but we have no choice. The product is almost ready for delivery." He nodded twice. "See that you do."

David clinched his teeth in an effort to control the renewed pulsing in his jaw. He snapped the phone shut and hooked it back on his belt. Then he closed the magazine and leaned forward to slip it under the driver's seat. When he did, a cut-out photograph of a nude female figure fell from the pages. He picked up the picture and his mood changed. He considered it briefly, then smiled, kissed it and slid it carefully into his inside coat pocket.

Jennifer stopped the red Miata beside Jonathan's car and turned off the ignition. On the other side of his Toyota was a well-worn Chevy van that she assumed belonged to Fenton Longstreet. At least it fit the description Jonathan had given her. She was relieved that they had arrived ahead of her and she would not have to sit and wait at an empty table. Tonight she wanted to spend as little time alone as possible. *Thank God for Jonathan and Margo,* she thought.

The session had been painful, but Margo's psychic surgery had been sensitive and skillful, and Jennifer felt for the first time since her childhood she had a chance to begin the healing process. Now, if Fenton could find some way to exorcise the virus, maybe she could banish the fear and learn to sleep again.

Jonathan had been careful to explain Fenton's situation. He had covered everything: the drinking, the divorce, the gypsy lifestyle, their enduring friendship since college days, everything. Jonathan wanted her to be able to make an objective, informed decision. But what were her options? Besides, Jonathan had pointed out that, before his fall, Fenton had been the rising star in one of the top legal firms in the Southeast. He was a bulldog in the courtroom. He would represent her for court costs and she could always terminate the relationship if it didn't work out. On top of that, Margo had also recommended she seek legal advice. But the bottom line was she was at the end of her rope.

Jennifer locked the Miata and headed for the pub's mahogany and brass entrance. Jonathan had suggested the watering hole as a neutral meeting ground. It was off the beaten path and they would be anonymous. If it didn't work out, they would have at least had a good drink, and he was buying. What did she have to lose that she hadn't already lost? She took a deep breath and opened the door. Right now she could use a good drink.

Jonathan stood up as Jennifer approached the table. "Hi, Jennifer," he said and reached out his hand, but she slipped past it and greeted him with a hug. "What would I do without you?" she whispered.

When she released him, he kept his arm around her and turned to Fenton who was standing holding his napkin.

"Jennifer, I'd like you to meet Fenton Longstreet. Fent, Jennifer Mitford."

After he completed the introductions and Jennifer was seated, Jonathan nodded to a waitress.

"We got a head start. What would you like to drink?" he asked.

Jennifer glanced at Fenton.

"It's okay." Fenton lifted his glass. "Jonathan's having a vodka tonic and I'm having a Coke."

Jennifer blushed slightly then turned to the waitress. "I'll have a gin and tonic."

"We took the liberty of ordering an appetizer. Jonathan remembered you like quesadillas," Fenton said.

"That sounds wonderful." Jennifer attempted a smile and unfolded her napkin as the waitress set her drink on the table along with a plate of quesadillas.

"How was Margo?" Jonathan asked.

Jennifer sipped the gin and closed her eyes.

"It's all right. I've told Fent everything you shared with me, so you won't have to go back through it again tonight," Jonathan said gently.

Jennifer laid her hand on his arm. It was more a gesture of exhaustion than affection.

"It was painful, but Margo was wonderful. I think there may be hope if Fent can keep David away from me." She opened her eyes and looked at Fenton. "Is that possible, Fent? Can you keep David away from me?"

Fenton had been following the conversation intently. "Jennifer, I can't even imagine what this must have been like for you," he said quietly.

He leaned forward as if reaching out for her.

"Since Jonathan and I talked I've been thinking about your situation and, yes, I think I can help you. I don't think there's any question that there is sufficient cause for a court order to keep David away from you. But—"

Fenton paused and Jonathan sensed he had come to a decision.

"I would also like to explore some other possibilities. Either way, you and I need to talk again. If you are interested in having me work with you perhaps we could meet tomorrow after you've had a chance to get a good night's rest."

Jennifer held tightly to her drink with one hand. Her other hand still rested on Jonathan's arm, but her weary eyes never left Fenton's.

"Yes, I would like that," she said.

Then she turned to Jonathan. "Jonathan, there's one very important thing I haven't told you, but now I must if Fenton is stepping into this thing. And I think you'll understand why it cannot leave this table, at least for now."

Jonathan felt a shiver in Jennifer's fingers.

"You know InterTel." It was more of a statement than a question.

"Yes," he answered. "That's the company that's merging with SatCom." He looked at her questioningly. Her fingers tightened on his arm.

"David is the Chief Financial Officer of InterTel. That's how he found me," she said with a note of finality.

Landon paused the VCR, freezing the actors on the monitor in a close-up of frenzied testosterone and lip-gloss, then reached for his cell phone.

"Hello, my man. This is a pleasant surprise. Didn't expect to hear from you until day after tomorrow."

He pushed the remains of his half-eaten Vegetarian Delite out of the way, propped his feet on the desk and leaned back. He switched hands with the phone and clicked off the VCR with a remote control.

"I'm working late. Had an endless editing session and I'm back in the office running through some transfers. How is it on your edge of the world?"

There was a long silence, and then an expression of deep concern lined Landon's face. He sat up and rolled to the desk, where he picked up a pen and started making notes on his appointment calendar.

"Jon, I'm terribly sorry to hear that. Absolutely. I understand completely. Take as much time as you need. Yes." He drew a circle. "I've got the phone number and your e-mail address. And you think you'll be back in the country toward the end of next week?"

He shook his head. "I appreciate it, but you don't have to do that. We'll muddle through."

He made another note. "Okay, amigo, you win. I'll check my e-mail in the morning. Remember me to your parents, and Jon, take care of yourself."

Landon laid the cell phone on the desk and stared at the blank screen on the video monitor. *Shit,* he thought. *When I was twenty-one, I thought I had it all figured out.*

Jonathan put down the phone and picked up Hemingway. He stroked him behind the ears and Hemingway broke into a deep baritone purr. *I'd better call Delta and see if I can get on the Friday morning non-stop to Tokyo-Narita. Then I need to e-mail Fent and get Lotus Matrix off to Landon, then tomorrow—Damn,* he thought. He began rummaging in his desk for paper and a pen. *I'd better make a list or I'll never get out of here.*

The message from his mother had been waiting on his answering machine when he got in from the meeting with Jennifer and Fent. An urgently blinking red light had announced its presence.

(pause) "Jonathan, when you get in would you give me a call? There's something I need to talk with you about. (pause) I'll be home for the next couple of hours. (pause) I love you."

Jonathan played the message three times. Maybe it was because he was worn out from the evening's emotional roller coaster, but there was something in his mother's voice that disturbed him. He finally decided it was the way she had said *"I love you."* There was the same conflicting mix of loss, hope and trepidation he remembered when she left him on his first day of kindergarten. Even at that tender age he sensed that an abiding love was the source of her turmoil, and it had sustained him. He picked up the phone and dialed.

"Hi, Mom, it's me. Just got in and picked up your message. Is everything okay?" he asked cautiously.

"Oh, Jonathan," she replied. "I'm so glad you called."

She hesitated, and Jonathan sensed that she was searching for words.

"First, I want you to know that we're okay." She paused and again he felt the hesitancy in her voice. "Your father is having some heart problems, but he's in the hospital and resting well."

"Dad's in the hospital with heart problems?" He tried not to let the shock show in his voice, but he knew he hadn't been successful.

"I know this comes as a dreadful surprise, but the doctors are very pleased with the way he's doing, and they think he should be back on his feet in no time," she said hopefully.

"God, Mom, how are *you* doing?" This time he didn't try to conceal the concern in his voice.

"It's been a little crazy and I'm tired, but other than that I'm doing okay. Everybody has been so kind."

Hemingway had stopped purring, but remained curled tightly in Jonathan's lap. Jonathan could feel his pulse rate starting to stabilize.

"When did it happen?" he asked.

"He began to feel uncomfortable after dinner last night. At first he thought it was just indigestion, but later the pain got worse, and he began to perspire and felt nauseated. That's when I called our doctor and he immediately sent an ambulance."

"Is he getting good medical care?" Jonathan could feel his own chest tightening.

"He's still in the CCU, but he's stable and the care has been wonderful. You know the Japanese, very attentive and professional. But, somehow, Mr. Takamoto found out about it and you would think your father was the Prime Minister. We have the top specialists and the hospital staff falling all over us. A housekeeper and special food have even been sent to the house."

Jonathan took his first complete breath since the beginning of the conversation. "That must be very comforting. I knew he and Takamoto-*san* were close, but that's amazing. What's the prognosis?"

"As I understand it, there was a small amount of damage to the heart muscle, but no blockage. He was fibrillating which led to arrhythmia, so in a few days they will put in a pacemaker to smooth things out, then, if all goes well, a couple of days after that he will come home. He'll have to take it easy for two weeks, then he should be as good as new, maybe even better with the pacemaker keeping tabs on things."

"Mom, that's very encouraging. How are Dad's spirits?" Jonathan could feel Hemingway relax as he fell asleep.

"You know your father—unsinkable. The nurses love him. In a way, he's kept me going," she said, her voice lifting.

Jonathan turned the pages of a small desk calendar lying beside the phone. He had made the decision the moment he recovered from his initial shock.

"Mom, I'm coming over. I'll get things squared away at the office tomorrow and can catch a plane out Friday. I'll be there on Saturday."

She didn't attempt to argue. "Can you do that on such short notice?" The relief in her voice was palpable.

"Sure. I can work it out. Right now I need to be with you and Dad."

"I don't think I'll be able to pick you up at the airport."

"That's okay. I don't want you to make that drive. I'll catch the train out of Narita. We'll have dinner and a glass of wine and then go see Dad."

"Oh, Jonathan, that sounds so wonderful." For the first time her voice betrayed her and he knew the tears were flowing.

"Thank you so much."

Jonathan felt his throat choke. "I love you, Mom," he said. "Give my love to Dad."

"Call me when your plane gets in, honey."

"I will, Mom. See you Saturday evening."

Jonathan laid the pen down and studied his list. The ticket, Fent, and getting the story synopsis off to Landon were things he could do tonight. The office stuff he, Mildred and Jennifer could work out in the morning. Stanley would probably get his shorts in a wad, but he'd get over it. The bright spot was dinner with Margo. Two hours with her was better than six hours in the lotus position and, he realized, before Thursday was over he might need both.

He eased Hemingway off his lap and unbagged the computer. Before he called Delta he thought he'd do a quick ticket price check on the Internet. Since it was last minute and there was only one non-stop, he knew he'd probably have to pay a premium, but it might give him something to talk about with the ticket agent.

"Damn, not again," Jonathan exhaled wearily when the desktop had loaded. A new file was waiting in its now customary place next to *My Documents*. It was titled *Near but too Far*.

He clicked and the icon opened.

Interrupted song
The nightingale distressed
Sheds a tear of love

Jonathan stared at the message. *How did she know?* he wondered. But his irritation had eased and he felt strangely comforted.

CHAPTER 10

*In the silver darkness of
dreams the green-ice waves close
over me once again.*

*I plunge deep past the
white corpse of the bellied up hull,
lungs on fire, searching through swollen
shadows of choked rigging and sails,
still clutching your glove,
frantic for a flicker of life.*

Margo put her chopsticks down, folded the poem and slipped it
into her pocket.

"I think you're getting close. How many more verses have you got
left?" she asked.

Jonathan slowly sipped his sake and let the hot fluid burn an
incandescent ribbon of relief through his beleaguered nervous
system. A day of balancing the demands of conflicting needs and
expectations, and arranging to get out of town had taken its toll.

As he had expected, Stanley had been a pain in the butt, but
Mildred and Jennifer had closed ranks and gone to bat for him. By
late afternoon the Great One had grudgingly come around. In fact, as
Jonathan was leaving, Stanley had even come out of his office to
wish him a safe trip.

Jonathan tasted the sake again and then set the cup carefully on
the table.

"You're right about the verses. Maybe two. Maybe only one. But, I'm going to have to put it aside for a while, at least until I get back from Japan."

Margo nodded. "It may be time for a break anyway. You really have a full plate right now and you need to save what energy you have for your parents. Besides," she smiled tenderly, "everything is working out just the way it's supposed to."

Jonathan sighed. They had been through this "like it's supposed to" stuff before and, although he generally accepted the idea, he was having a hard time buying it tonight.

"If you say so," he reluctantly agreed. Under the circumstances it was the best he could do with it.

Her eyes accepted his exhausted psyche and then released him. "Maybe when you've returned and had a chance to catch your breath. How is Jennifer doing?" she asked.

"She seemed in better spirits today. She's retained Fent to straighten out this mess with her stepfather."

Margo nibbled on her sushi. "That's quite a step for Fent, isn't it?"

"Yeah, it really is. I wasn't sure he would do it, but I think we can thank the Dragon Lady for that. She's the one who brought him in from the cold." The sake was doing its job.

"Everything's happening—"

Jonathan held up his hand. "I know. Just like it's supposed to."

Margo smiled. "What's the latest on the mysterious Dragon Lady?" she asked.

"Her last haiku was very touching, even comforting, but the odd thing is she knew something had happened in Japan before I told anybody. It was almost as if she knew before I did."

"That is peculiar. I guess I'd better put on my flight suit and get to work. Fent hasn't been able to find anything that would be of help, has he?" she asked.

"No, the trail's cold, not that it was ever hot, and now he has his hands full with Jennifer."

"Feast or famine. I'll see what I can do." She hesitated,

momentarily lost in thought. "Do you know anyone who uses Shalimar perfume?"

Jonathan looked at her curiously. "Other than you? No, I don't think so, why?"

"Just thinking of someone I ran into."

Jonathan nodded. "It's a nice fragrance."

"Yes, it is." Margo changed the subject. "How did Landon take postponing a decision?"

Jonathan drained the last tiny cup of sake and took a final bite of sushi. "He was understanding and very supportive. Of course, I sent him Lotus Matrix as a sweetener."

Margo folded her napkin and sat back. "So, it looks like you've covered all the bases. How much packing do you have to do?" she asked.

"Not much. It's a short trip and I travel pretty light."

"Do you need help with Hemingway?"

"I dropped him off with Jennifer over lunch, but thanks for asking."

Margo reached across the table and took his hand. "Take care of yourself, Jonathan. You know how much I love you."

Jonathan took her other hand. "And I you, Margo-*san. Kokoro wo komete.*"

Part II

CHAPTER 11

After the desolate expanse of the Bering Sea, the lush foliage of the Japanese islands sparkled like emeralds scattered in a Zen rock garden. Jonathan turned from the window and adjusted his seat belt as the Delta jet dropped through six thousand feet on its final approach into Tokyo's Narita International Airport.

"I hope your father finds good health, Jonathan-*san*." The young Japanese girl seated next to him smiled shyly and closed her notebook.

Jonathan returned her smile. "Thank you Kumi-*san*. You're very kind." He nodded toward the notebook she was stuffing in her small backpack. "I hope you pass your English test. Five hundred words is a lot to learn in one summer."

Kumi slid the pack under the seat. "Thank you for helping me practice."

"*Doo itashimashite*. It was my pleasure. Is someone meeting you at Narita?"

"Yes. My grandmother will be there. She is driving from Kawasaki."

Jonathan laughed. "She must have great courage."

Kumi's eyes twinkled. "Yes. She likes big adventure."

They were interrupted by the hydraulic whine and thump of the landing gear being lowered.

Jonathan looked back out the window at the landscape flashing past. "We're almost there."

Kumi leaned forward to see. "Yes, almost home."

Twenty-five minutes later Jonathan rolled his bag out of customs. On his two previous visits his parents had picked him up, so he had never taken the train out of the airport. He had no doubt that he could handle the complex Tokyo metro area system, but the fatigue of the fourteen-hour flight was catching up with him, so he stepped out of the surging crowd to catch his breath and sort through his shoulder bag for a railway map.

"Excuse me, but are you Mr. Jonathan Livingson?"

Jonathan looked up to see a young Japanese businessman in his signature black suit standing before him holding a card with his name on it.

"Why, yes I am," Jonathan said in surprise.

The businessman bowed slightly. "I am Yoshida Hiroshi. I have been sent by Mr. Takamoto to pick you up and take you to your parents' home."

Jonathan attempted to bow and the strap of his shoulder bag slipped off his shoulder. Before he could regain control Yoshida stepped forward and caught it.

"Let me help you with your bag, Livingson-*san*."

"Thank you. I'm afraid I'm a little tired," Jonathan confessed and completed an awkward bow.

"I understand." Yoshida acknowledged the bow. "It is a very long flight."

"Your English is excellent, Yoshida-*san*," Jonathan said, regaining his composure.

Yoshida smiled. "Thank you. Georgia Tech, class of ninety-three. Major in Computer Technology and a minor in Industrial Management. I understand your Japanese is likewise excellent. Are these your only bags?"

"Yes, they are."

"Allow me."

They started walking toward the exit, Yoshida carrying the shoulder bag and pulling the roll-on.

"But you say you went to Georgia Tech? This is an unexpected surprise," Jonathan said.

THE CHANDANA TREE

"Yes. That's why Takamoto-*san* sent me. He thought it would be comforting if someone from home met you."

"Takamoto-*san* is very thoughtful."

"He is the reason I left the States and returned to Japan."

They had left the terminal and were crossing the sidewalk toward a black Mercedes. Jonathan hesitated when they approached the car. Yoshida laughed. "Don't worry. I know what you're thinking and it's not Yakuza. The gangsters do drive these things, and people do get out of the way when they see it coming, which embarrasses Takamoto-*san*. But we use it for visiting dignitaries, and it was the only car left in the pool when I checked out this morning." Yoshida looked at his watch. "With any luck we'll beat the rush hour and I'll have you at your parents' home in two hours, in plenty of time for that glass of wine you're planning to have with your mother."

Jonathan looked quizzically at Yoshida.

Yoshida smiled. "Your father told Takamoto-*san* that you and your mother are planning to have wine and dinner before going to the hospital." Yoshida opened the trunk of the Mercedes and gestured. "So, as he instructed, I have brought a case of Pinot Noir for you from our vineyards in France. As you can see, Takamoto-*san* thinks of everything."

"I think that's an understatement. I continue to be impressed."

Ten minutes later Yoshida had maneuvered through the Narita traffic and entered the Higashi-Kanto Expressway for Tokyo.

Jonathan settled back in the comfortable leather seat. *This mode of transportation is certainly luxurious*, he thought. It was a far cry from the tiring and crowded train trip he had prepared himself for. And, as an added benefit, he realized that he had taken an immediate liking to the thoughtful and helpful Yoshida. He turned to his host.

"Tell me, Yoshida-*san*, what sort of work do you do at Takamoto International?" he asked.

"I handle special projects for Takamoto-*san*."

They had entered a toll plaza. Yoshida stopped at a toll booth, received a ticket from the uniformed attendant, then accelerated back into the traffic flow.

"That sounds interesting."

Yoshida smiled. "Especially when it's a visiting American writer from Atlanta."

"I'm a project? I thought you were just picking me up," Jonathan said, amused.

"Crossing the street is a project at Takamoto International. Nothing is left to chance, and you've gotten the full treatment." Yoshida tapped a file folder beside him on the seat. "It's all here in my briefing papers: family history, education, professional career, the works. By the way," he asked, "did you enjoy your five years in Japan?"

"Why, yes I did," Jonathan said, the amusement turning to dismay.

"One thing though, we could use a more recent picture of you. I had a hard time picking you out in the crowd."

Yoshida reached into the file, pulled out a photograph and handed it to Jonathan.

Jonathan took the picture and stared at the image in disbelief. His chest tightened and the wet taste of death backed up in his throat. She was there in his arms. They were dressed in tee shirts and shorts and were standing on the deck of a sailboat. Her head was on his shoulder and she was laughing as he kissed her cheek. A gust of wind had just caught her hair, casting it before the sun like a net of golden flax. Its summer-mown fragrance enveloped him once again and he felt his lips tracing her eyes and the arch of her neck. Then he saw her pulling him down and wrapping a tanned leg around him as he released himself into the sanctuary of her magic, burrowing deeper into the boundless mystery of their passion.

He could barely speak. "This was six years ago. How did you get—?"

Yoshida immediately sensed Jonathan's consternation. "I hope I have not offended you in some way, Livingson-*san*." He glanced at Jonathan anxiously. "My understanding is this is a photograph your family gave Takamoto-*san*. Because of his long relationship with your father and the affection he has for your family, I am of the impression he considers you almost as a son. I assure you his interest is the highest of compliments."

Yoshida hesitated as if testing his footing. "Also, you should know that the information in this file is only general in nature. I know nothing of the details of your personal life," he said cautiously.

Jonathan came up for air, pushed the waves aside and handed the photo back to Yoshida. "Thank you for your concern, Yoshida-*san*." He attempted to regain his composure. "The picture just took me by surprise." He managed a weak smile. "I am complimented by Takamoto-*san*'s gracious interest."

Yoshida appeared relieved that the crisis had passed. "There is one other thing," he said thoughtfully. "Although twelve years separate us, I think we have perhaps both felt the chill of the northeast wind. I, too, was born under the sign of the tiger."

Landon sat in a secluded corner of the juice bar munching granola and studying several typewritten pages spread out on the table before him. It was early and the morning light floated, suspended from the bright hibiscus sheltering the patio as if waiting for its next cue. It was Landon's favorite time. The juice jockeys weren't in yet and he had the place to himself, which gave him a chance to catch his breath and get his bearings before plunging into another day of smoke and mirrors. The frisky little blonde wouldn't be in until ten-thirty, which today was all right with him. Today he had plenty to focus on and, he thought, as he thumbed through the sheets before him, the day was looking better by the page.

Landon sipped his apricot tea and made a few notes, then picked up his cell phone and dialed.

"Peter, my man. I know it's early, but I woke up around five and couldn't get back to sleep, so I came down to Papaya Paradise for an early start. Did you get my e-mail?" He made another note and a slow smile navigated the tanned character lines of his face.

"I know, I know. There is a God. Jonathan may have just saved our lives," he exclaimed, then pushed the bowl of granola out of the way and picked up the papers.

"I completely agree, amigo. The mix of fantasy and reality is hot, and Nishikawa is going to love the tie-in with Eastern philosophy."

For the first time in weeks Landon felt a tentative spark ignite in his solar plexus. "The story and special effects possibilities are unlimited." The spark became a flicker. He nodded and shuffled through the pages.

"Page four. I've got it." He listened, following along on the page. "You are absolutely right, Peter." The flicker became a flame. "The spin-off into computer gaming and interactive makes Lotus Matrix one hell of a crossover package. It's a marketing and promotional dream."

Landon paused, and a more sober note entered his voice. "That is if Nishikawa and Takamoto sign on. How was your afternoon with the financial people yesterday?" he asked warily.

A cloud darkened his face. "So, it's that bad."

He slumped forward on the table for support while he listened. "So, unless Takamoto picks up his option, the party's over even before Abracadabra has a chance to turn things around."

Landon was silent. The flame began to flicker. Finally he leaned back. "Okay, pardner. We have Jonathan's proposal and God knows whatever else we can put together, and we've got one day to do it. We've done it before, Peter, and we can do it again. Let's saddle up and kick ass."

Jonathan's mother adjusted the flower arrangement on the dining table, then placed a plate of red bean cakes and two napkins beside it.

"They put the pacemaker in this morning and from what the doctors say everything went perfectly. It's already working and your father is resting comfortably." She smiled optimistically. "I just think it's a miracle what they can do these days."

Jonathan filled her wine glass as she smoothed her skirt and settled into a chair opposite him. After their initial hug it was their first quiet moment together since Yoshida had assured himself that he could be of no further assistance. Jonathan had offered him a glass of wine, but Yoshida graciously insisted that he should check in at the office and must be on his way.

Jonathan could see the fatigue in his mother's deep olive eyes, but he knew it was only a temporary concession by her indomitable spirit to the demands of the past few days. *In fact*, he thought, *crises have always served her well. She's never more beautiful than when the greatest demands are being made of her; as if she finds the sweetest water when she has to dip into the deepest part of the well.*

"You're beautiful, Mom. I hope you know that."

"Jonathan," her eyes became damp and she made no attempt to hide her emotion. "I'm so glad you're here. It's such a very long way." She took a handkerchief from her skirt pocket and dabbed her eyes. "How was your flight?"

"You know how much I love you." He reached out and squeezed her hand.

"I feel it even from so far away." They continued to hold onto each other.

"The flight was fine. Long, as always, but I had a pleasant seat companion which helped pass the hours." He released her hand and sipped his wine. "This is very good wine. Takamoto-*san* doesn't miss a beat, does he?"

"No, he doesn't. He has been a great support. His people are everywhere and he thinks of everything. This would have been much more difficult without his kindness."

"And you continue to be satisfied with the medical attention Dad's getting?"

"Oh, my, yes. The surgeon who did the procedure today was typical. He just couldn't have been more helpful. Of course it helps to be fluent in the language. At least I can keep up with what everyone is saying."

"I'm sure that works both ways. You said Dad is resting comfortably. Do you think I could see him tonight?" He looked at his watch. "It's almost dinnertime now."

"The hospital is about a thirty-minute drive depending on traffic on highway sixteen. Why don't I fix something to eat, then we'll run up there and poke our heads in for a few minutes. He's anxious to see you." She got up and began clearing the table.

Jonathan stood up to help her. "You're not cooking tonight. You must have a favorite place nearby and I'm taking you out for dinner."

She started to protest but Jonathan interrupted. "None of that now. I'm here to help." He put his arm around her. "And I want you to be thinking of anything else I can do to make your life a little easier."

She turned in his arm and held him. "Dinner out would be nice. Do you remember the little sushiya down near the water in Kanagawa? We went there for your high school graduation."

"I remember. It had a blue noren above the door and looked out over a small marina. I really loved that place."

"Well, it's still there run by the same family, only the younger generation has taken over and turned it into a health food restaurant. It's awesome."

Jonathan laughed. "It's awesome?"

Her eyes shimmered. "Isn't that what the young people say these days? Please tell me I'm not losing complete touch."

Jonathan kissed her. "You're not losing touch. I don't know what they're saying in Japan, but you're right on for an American gaijin."

She returned the kiss then turned to the sink to wash the wine glasses while Jonathan wrapped up the remaining red bean cakes and put them in the refrigerator.

"There is one small favor I wonder if I might ask." She adjusted the hot and cold water.

"Sure, anything."

"Before your father's heart acted up, I had planned lunch with a young lady at an art gallery in Kamakura to pick up a small ceramic figurine. It was to be a match for one I had already purchased, but I cancelled when we had to dash to the hospital." She handed a wet wine glass and dishtowel to Jonathan.

"Anyway, to make a long story short, Mr. and Mrs. Takamoto have invited you and me to dinner in Yokohama tomorrow night, and I would like to take the figurine to them as a gift of appreciation for all they have done. Mr. Takamoto is coming to visit your father over lunch tomorrow, so I rescheduled lunch at the gallery for that time. The only problem is my Fujinkai—my neighborhood wives group—called an impromptu meeting for the same time. I would skip it, but I think they are planning something special for me, and they have been so kind to include me, and so very supportive through this whole thing it would be out of the question not to attend. So, I was wondering if, after you see your father in the morning, could you run over to Kamakura, take the young lady to lunch and pick up the figurine?"

Jonathan finished drying the second glass. "Where do you keep the wine glasses?"

"In the cabinet next to the stove."

"What's the lady's name?"

"Naoko Matsuzawa, and she's quite pretty."

Jonathan put the glasses in the cabinet. "You say she's pretty?"

His mother blushed slightly. "Well, yes, you know...." She smiled at him hopefully.

Jonathan shook his head. "You're so transparent. There's not a devious bone in your body." Then he grinned and kissed her. "Sure, Mom, I'll be glad to."

CHAPTER 12

Fenton frowned and put the handset back in the pay phone cradle. *That's very strange,* he thought. He held the napkin up to the light and studied the phone number written on it. *I'm sure this is the right number. I checked it with her twice. Jennifer said David Finley's instructions were to call this number and leave a message if she wanted to get in touch. Maybe I misdialed.* Fenton dug in his pocket, pulled out thirty-five cents, plugged it into the phone and carefully redialed the number.

After the fourth ring the same female voice answered. "This is NuTech Services. I'm sorry we are not available at the moment, but your call is important to us—"

Fenton hung up. *What, or who the hell is Nu Tech Services, and why would he give Jennifer that number?* he wondered. He looked at his watch. *And, you'd think somebody would be there at two-thirty in the afternoon,* he thought. He needed a few minutes on R2D2. He put the napkin in his pocket, picked up the tattered briefcase, squeezed between the wrought iron benches and crossed the sidewalk to the café.

The follow-up meeting with Jennifer had gone well. She had been relaxed and, although Fenton knew it was painful, she responded openly to his questions. Other than the phone number David had given her, she was not able to provide much in the way of new information, but the bruised and battered old bulldog in him had listened carefully to the anguish constricting her words, and by the time their meeting was over he had kicked out the cobwebs and was ready to rumble.

As a concession to his re-entry into the real world Fenton had bought a cell phone. But he was careful to point out to Jennifer that its sole purpose was for communicating with her in case of an emergency. She was the only one with the number, and it was to be used only if David appeared or contacted her; otherwise, they would communicate via the Internet. The existence of the café he kept a secret. Her case was a test run, and he wasn't about to reveal the presence of his safe house. He was throwing the bulldog a bone, and only time would tell if he still had any teeth. If it didn't work out, he could cancel the cell phone, drop back out and no one would be the wiser.

Whatever the outcome, it's nice to help a pretty, no, make that very pretty lady in distress, he thought, as he settled down in front of R2D2 and punched into *atlantabusinesssearch.com.* He was waiting for the website to open when a voice announced: "You have mail." He clicked on the *Mail* button and the window opened. He had one message from: *jnightingale. Subject: Search at home.*

"Son of a bitch," he exclaimed. He double-clicked and the message opened.

The foul mynah bird
A petty chieftain his nest
For greed defiling

So, she's back in action, he thought. Then he noticed that, like her first message on Jonathan's computer, there was space on the scroll bar so he pulled it down and one more line appeared. *The Dragon Lady* was centered in the page in a neat, feminine script.

Damn, she's slick. Looks like she's picked our pockets again, he thought.

He returned to the message: Mynah bird, chief, nest defiles. Birds of a feather, flock together, he mused. He pondered its meaning, then took a pen from the inside pocket of the Harris Tweed and started doodling while R2D2 finished loading the Atlanta Business Search database.

Jonathan bowed to the woman who greeted him as he stepped through the door of Shiki Gallery. *"Watashi wa Jonathan Livingson to mooshimasu ga. Matsuzawa-san irrashaimasu ka?"*

The woman returned his bow. "Yes, Livingson-*san*, Matsuzawa-*san* is here. I am Maeda Yuki," she answered in flawless English.

It was apparent to Jonathan she was expecting him. "Please, make yourself at home. I will get her."

At that moment a young woman stepped through an office door at the back of the gallery. She was dressed in a black cotton jacket, a white vee-necked blouse and a dark maroon print skirt. But it was her face that took Jonathan's breath. Framed by her dark hair, it conveyed the mystery and magic of the ancient prints of geishas he had fallen in love with in his youth, now come alive, thoroughly modern, delicate, fresh and expectant. She hesitated when their eyes met and her lips parted slightly as if in secret recognition.

The woman turned to her. "Matsuzawa-*san*, this is Jonathan Livingson-*san*."

Naoko's eyes fluttered and she bowed. "I am honored to meet you, Livingson-*san*." Her voice was like a temple chime.

My God, she is beautiful, Jonathan thought, and bowed. "I, too, am honored, Matsuzawa-*san*."

Naoko looked up. Her eyes held his. "Your mother called this morning and explained your coming. How is father's health?" she asked.

"You are kind to ask. I saw him this morning and he is doing very well." He was captured by the cautious embrace of her eyes. "The doctors think he will be able to come home soon."

"I am most happy for your good news." She smiled modestly, then turned to the check-out counter where a box was wrapped and tied with a raffia bow. "We have figurine your mother ordered ready for you, Livingson-*san*."

"Thank you very much," Jonathan said. Suddenly, he was struck by an irrational fear that she was going to hand him the package and end their brief encounter. In a state of alarm he hesitated, at a loss for words, uncertain of how to proceed.

"I understand that you and Matsuzawa-*san* are to have lunch. Why don't you pick up the figurine when you return?" Yuki suggested, smiling first at him and then at Naoko.

Jonathan realized she had thrown him a life preserver. "Thank you, Maeda-*san*. Yes, I could do that," he said with relief. He turned to Naoko. "Do you have a favorite place to eat, Matsuzawa-*san*?" he asked.

Her eyes reflected his relief and she momentarily slipped back into Japanese. "*Arigatoo gozaimasu.*" Then she caught herself, put her hand to her face and blushed. "Thank you for your kindness, Livingson-*san*. There is small *sobaya* short walk on this street. It is very good."

Jonathan nodded. "That sounds very nice. I would enjoy soba."

"Then we will go," she said, obviously pleased. She turned and bowed slightly to Yuki. "We will not be away long."

"Take your time." Yuki smiled at Jonathan. "Livingson-*san* is an important customer." Then she bowed. "It was a pleasure to meet you."

"The pleasure is all mine, Maeda-*san*. You have a beautiful gallery." Jonathan bowed, then turned and held the door open for Naoko.

"Enjoy your lunch," Yuki called after them as they stepped into the crowded street.

Ten minutes later, Jonathan and Naoko had left the bustle of the busy street behind and were seated at one of six tables in the tiny soba restaurant Naoko had suggested. Jonathan was enchanted.

They had found the entrance at the end of a narrow, gray cedar plank and grass walkway that was screened from the shops on either side by low stone walls, topped by dark brown lattice and slat privacy fences. The approach appeared to have been carefully designed to create an inviting transition from the distractions and turmoil of the street. Overhanging trees enveloped the path with the fragrance of juniper, and the way was marked by small iron lanterns. A maroon noren cloth with the restaurant's symbol and name in kanji characters hung from a beam beneath the brown tile roof that sheltered the entrance. A stone lantern stood to the left of the door in a meticulously manicured clump of bamboo, and a small window with samples of the restaurant's fare was to the right. The thoughtfully arranged elements created a suspended, timeless mood of serene intimacy.

Inside, the walls were white and decorated with Zen ink paintings and Hokusai prints of Mount Fuji. A tatami room for private parties was to their right, complete with sandals neatly lined up by its shoji paper doors. Behind Naoko was a diminutive stone garden, shaded by bamboo and a dwarf red maple tree. In the background, *koto* music played softly from an unseen audio system.

Jonathan sipped his green tea. "It's nice to be back in Japan, Matsuzawa-*san*. I had no idea how much I have missed your country. I feel as if I am home."

"Thank you, Livingson-*san*. When were you last here?" she asked.

"It has been five years since my last trip," he replied.

"Someday I hope to visit your country," she said, her eyes unlocked, drawing him in.

Jonathan was enthralled. She was irresistibly defenseless.

"I would be honored to show you some of my country," he said.

"If it pleases you, I can show you Kamakura. How long is your stay?"

"I am here for only a few days. I will be leaving when my father returns home from the hospital. I must return to my work," he said, regretfully.

A door closed and her eyes fell. "Yes, I understand work. It is important."

"I have just a short time." The panic he felt in the gallery was returning.

"May I ask question?" she asked tentatively.

He nodded. "Yes, of course."

Her eye lashes fluttered, catching the light like dragonfly wings.

"If we were in America now, what name would you call me?" she asked.

"Most of the time in America we use our given names, not our family names."

"Then I would call you Jonathan?"

"Yes, and I would call you Naoko."

She nodded almost imperceptibly, then, the barest hint of a smile touched her lips and her eyes opened to him again. "I like that, Jonathan."

Jonathan felt his heart stop. "So do I, Naoko."

Margo stopped in mid-sentence, transfixed.

"Margo, are you alright?" Jennifer asked.

The wind had suddenly come up, taking her completely by surprise, but this time instead of being accompanied by breaking surf, it was the sound of wind in a forest. Margo raised her hand, as if to say, *just a moment*, then got up and went to the window, pulled the curtain back and stared into the night. She closed her eyes trying to determine the source, but the initial gusts were already beginning to diminish. Then, just before the last whisper faded, she distinctly heard the dancing of a leaf and the contemplative song of a *koto*. *It's from the East,* she thought. She listened a few seconds longer, then smiled, closed the curtain and returned to her seat facing Jennifer.

Jennifer was watching her closely. "You went somewhere, didn't you?" she asked.

Margo settled back into their space. "Are you familiar with Chaos Theory?" she asked.

"You mean the idea that when a butterfly in Australia flutters its wings, it causes something to happen in the Norwegian Parliament?"

"Yes, more or less."

"Jonathan and I did some research on it for an article in the SatCom magazine."

Margo nodded. "Sometimes I get caught in the matrix between the butterfly and the end result."

"Can you tell what the end result will be?"

Margo shook her head and raised a finger. "Remember, I'm not a fortune teller."

"No. But maybe you're my butterfly," Jennifer said quietly.

The hushed, new age music embraced them, then she smiled sadly and her eyes fell.

"Have you heard anymore from David?" Margo asked gently.

"No, it's been quiet, thank God. But I think it's because he's so tied up in this merger right now. I heard he was interviewed on a CNN business program last night."

"Are you satisfied with the way things are going with Fenton?"

Jennifer nodded. "Yes." She shifted in her chair and leaned forward. "For now we've decided not to get a restraining order. The merger is complicating everything, and if our history came out right now it would be my word against his, and David is a powerful man and a pathological liar. Because of his position, the media would be all over it, and right now I don't think I could take the public humiliation."

Margo was taking notes while she listened. "I understand. There are some issues here that we need to come back to, but first, I'm concerned for your immediate safety. What does Fenton have in mind?"

"We've met with security at the Factory. They have given me an emergency beeper. All I have to do is press the button and they will be there. They are doubling their patrols and are now checking everyone at the gate around the clock, not just at night."

"How much did you tell them about David?"

"Nothing. As far as security is concerned I have had two attempted break-ins. Fent doesn't want to risk alerting David that anyone beyond house security is involved."

"I don't understand. Why not just call in the police?" Margo asked.

"Because Fent has stumbled onto something. He doesn't just want to restrain David, he wants to put him away for good, and he thinks he can do that without compromising me or my name."

Margo nodded thoughtfully. "But what if it doesn't work?"

Jennifer let out a breath of finality and shrugged. "Then we get a restraining order and you'll have to find some way to rescue me." They were both silently pondering that eventuality, when Jennifer spoke. "I almost forgot. Fent asked if you have a computer."

"Yes, I do."

She opened her purse and took out an envelope. "This sounds a little strange and he seemed embarrassed to be asking, but he said you would understand."

She handed the envelope to Margo. "He asked if the next time you are dragging the galaxy for the Dragon Lady, would you include this on your itinerary, and e-mail him if you make a contact."

Margo opened the envelope and unfolded a diagram drawn on a sheet of legal paper. In the center of the page was a circle labeled InterTel overlapping a square labeled SatCom. Beneath the two was the word Merger.

To the left of the Merger diagram was a triangle designated NuTech Services. Inside the triangle were two stick figures. One identified as David Finley and the other as Stanley Wiggins. Two arrows were drawn from the Merger diagram to the figures in the NuTech triangle, one arrow from InterTel and one from SatCom.

Above the Merger drawing and connected to InterTel with a line was a box with a name Margo recognized immediately: Takamoto International.

At the bottom of the page was an e-mail address: *junkdog@onlinecafe.com.*

Margo looked up at Jennifer. "Isn't Stanley Wiggins your and Jonathan's boss at SatCom?" she asked.

Jennifer nodded.

Margo stared at her. "I see." She studied the diagram again. "From this drawing it looks like Stanley and David may have something going on the side."

Jennifer nodded again. "That's what Fent's working on."

"This is getting very close to home."

"Yes, it is. I feel surrounded."

Margo carefully folded the diagram and slipped it into its envelope, then she looked back up at Jennifer. "Tell Junkdog it's in my flight bag."

She kept the Takamoto International connection to herself.

Jonathan stood looking out the window. From the second floor bedroom he could see down the narrow street of closely grouped, well-maintained homes. Their tile roofs glittered in the sun and their light colored walls formed a background for a variety of carefully pruned and sculpted foliage. On the far corner was a small park where children were playing on swings and a colorful climbing apparatus. Behind the house a ridge led up to a range of blue mountains that formed a buffer between the southern bay area and Yokohama, Tokyo, and the industrial regions to the north.

"You're sure Takamoto-*san* said casual?" he called out to his mother.

"Yes, dear. You don't have to worry about a suit and tie tonight," she replied from her bedroom where she was applying her final touches for the evening.

That's unusual, Jonathan thought. *But then, this trip has already turned out to be more than I'd expected.*

He was still under Naoko's spell, and she had left him locked in a Sumo match of conflicting emotions. He was at once exhilarated and cautious, entranced and mystified, but most troubling were the intimations of rapture he had felt in her presence.

"God," he muttered, "I promised myself I'd never let this happen to me again. Hemingway will never forgive me—"

"What time is it, Jonathan?" his mother called out.

Jonathan looked at his watch. "It's five-thirty."

"Oh, my, Yoshida-*san* will be here any minute."

But to his frustration, Naoko suffused him like an exotic incense from which his senses could not, or would not let go. He checked his watch again. *Damn, enough of this,* he thought. *I've got to finish getting ready.* He reached for his wallet and checked his pockets for loose change. When he did, his fingers found the gallery's card Naoko had handed him when he left. He took it out, turned it to the light, and admired the colorful graphic. *Very nice work,* he thought, then he turned it over. On the back Naoko's name and e-mail address were written in a delicate, flowing script. He was stunned. The graceful strokes of her pen were like incandescent meridians traced on the outer boundary of his heart. He surrendered. *Okay, to hell with it,* he decided. There could be nothing wrong with seeing her one more time. He stuffed the card back in his pocket. Then, he would get on the plane, and seven thousand miles later it would be over. But as he thought about leaving, the panic he had felt at lunch gripped him, and he knew that his and Hemingway's carefully guarded world was crumbling.

A knock on the door interrupted his speculations.

"That must be Yoshida-*san*," his mother said from the bedroom door.

Jonathan quickly gathered himself together. "I'll run down and let him in." He paused at the door and took her hands. "You look great," he said, then kissed her on the cheek before hurrying down the stairs.

CHAPTER 13

Landon sipped nervously from a can of Diet Cola and stared out his office window. He adjusted the blinds so he could see the bustle of activity one floor below on the main street of the Centurion Pictures lot. It was comforting to know that there were people in the business who still had work to do. He looked at his watch for the third time. It had been an hour and a half since Peter had left with Nishikawa for the airport, and with each passing minute his hopes were fading.

Landon looked at the Cola can in disgust. "Shit, I can't believe I'm drinking this stuff," he muttered. "We've got to get a different drink machine." He threw the can in a trash basket. "If Nishikawa doesn't get me, the fucking mutant toxins will."

In frustration he turned to his desk and picked up a bound copy of the proposal he and Peter had presented to Nishikawa three hours earlier. He had absolutely no idea how to evaluate the meeting. Phrases like, "polite friendly exchange," and "thoughtful, probing questions" came to mind but, beyond that, he was at a loss. If he had to sum it up, he had no idea what he would say. Nishikawa had maintained an impenetrable air of polite inscrutability. The only energy shift Landon thought he detected was when they presented Jonathan's *Lotus Matrix*. Nishikawa had leaned forward very slightly and Landon thought his right eyebrow twitched, but that was about it. *The man's a goddamn Buddha,* he thought.

Landon thumbed through the proposal one more time then returned to the window. A black limo inched along the street, weaving between electricians moving lights and set dressers carrying props into stage "B" across the way. Landon knew that three buildings away on stage "C" the set was being prepared for the last three episodes of what could be the end of his career. His world was collapsing, and he could see the final scene as the special effects kicked in, not in the form of a spectacular computer-generated cataclysm, but as a glutinous digital meltdown of the Wicked Witch of the North.

The walls were closing in. He wiped his forehead and attempted a deep breath. *I need fresh air. I've got to get out of here,* he decided. He took a folded piece of paper out of his pocket and read the inscription: *Penny 555-1006.* The cute little waitress at the juice bar had slipped him her phone number yesterday at lunch. He put the paper back in his pocket and picked up the desk phone.

"Ginger, I'm leaving for the day. When Peter calls, patch him through to my cell phone."

The black Mercedes turned onto a broad concrete pier thrusting into Yokohama Bay. "You continue to be a man of many surprises, Yoshida-*san,*" Jonathan said.

To his left he could see the huge Ferris wheel and Landmark Tower skyscraper that dominated the Yokohama waterfront and, in the distance to his right, the Yokohama Bay Bridge arched gracefully across the entrance to the harbor. In the gathering dusk, lights along the shore began to sparkle on the water, accented here and there by flashing pinpoints of red and green marking the safe lanes of shipping channels.

Yoshida smiled. "Since the last few days have been so stressful for you, Takamoto-*san* thought you might enjoy something a little more relaxing and refreshing this evening."

Just ahead, tied up to the right side of the pier, was a large, brightly lit cruise ship with passengers boarding. They passed a marine police station and passenger terminal, then he pulled the car to a stop beside a white uniformed attendant.

"This is where we get out."

"This is so exciting," his mother whispered as they stepped out of the car into the crisp evening sea breeze. "Don't forget our gift."

"I have it right here," Jonathan said reassuringly, and held it for her to see.

Yoshida spoke briefly to the attendant and handed him the car keys, then checked his watch and turned to Jonathan and his mother. "It looks like we're right on schedule. Why don't we go aboard?"

They maneuvered past the long line of passengers and were ushered up the gangway amid bows from the smiling and smartly uniformed crew. Once they were on board, an officer greeted Yoshida and led them up through three decks to a private dining room overlooking the main deck.

After the officer left, Jonathan turned to Yoshida. "You have a nice ship here."

"Yes, it meets our needs." He smiled. "I'm sure you and Livingson-*san* are curious."

"It's very beautiful." She looked out the window at the graceful superstructure delineated with colorful lights. "But, I hope we won't be gone too long. I only packed my handbag."

Yoshida laughed. "I think your handbag should be sufficient. The Royal Ark is a dinner cruise ship. It is one of four ships owned by Takamoto International. The others cruise long distance between ports in the islands. We will be out for several hours but will stay within the Yokohama Bay area. After dinner the crew will provide entertainment and lead dancing on the main deck. Dinner on the boat, as he refers to it, is one of the Takamoto-*san's* favorite diversions, and it is his hope that you will find the evening more relaxing than a more formal dinner ashore." Yoshida stepped closer and lowered his voice. "It's also a well known secret that Mrs. Takamoto loves to dance the Macarena and—"

At that moment the cabin door opened and the officer who had greeted them ushered in a smiling, middle-aged Japanese man dressed in deck shoes, gray slacks and a blue blazer over a pink polo shirt.

"Margaret-*san*, how good it is to see you again so soon," he exclaimed. "I trust that you have been able to get some rest." He then bowed slightly and extended his hand.

Mrs. Livingson took his hand and returned his bow. "Thank you, Takeo-*san*. Yes, because of your kind assistance I have had time to catch my breath."

"And you are Jonathan." Takamoto turned to Jonathan and extended his hand. "I have waited so long to see you again. I believe it has been almost twenty-three years."

Jonathan shook his hand and bowed slightly. "Thank you, Takamoto-*san*. Yes, I believe it was at my high school graduation." The handshake was firm and confident. In that instant Jonathan understood why Yoshida had chosen to return to Japan to work for Takamoto International.

"May I introduce my wife, Maeko." Takamoto turned and took the hand of a smiling, vivacious woman who had just stepped through the door.

She bowed. "Jonathan-*san*, how nice to meet you at last." Then she turned to Mrs. Livingson. "And, Margaret-*san*, I think of you so often."

Takamoto smiled, taking the hand of the young woman who followed. "And, I believe you both have met my daughter."

Naoko smiled and a soft flush of pink crept up her neck when her eyes met Jonathan's.

Jonathan was stunned, momentarily speechless.

"Oh, what a nice surprise! How good to see you again, Naoko-*san*," his mother effused.

Before Jonathan could catch his breath Yoshida appeared at the door. "Excuse me, everyone. The captain has just passed word that the passengers are all aboard and we are ready to depart."

Takamoto nodded with satisfaction. "Excellent. Be so kind as to extend my compliments to Captain Kimura, Yoshida-*san*." Then he turned to his guests. "Now, if you would join me at the table."

Dinner was a blur for Jonathan. He and Naoko were seated across from each other, and every time their eyes met he was sure everyone in the room could feel the multiple seismic tremors dancing back and forth across the gyoza and tempura. Somehow he was able to follow the course of conversation around the table and contribute when appropriate, but exchanges between them were limited to brief pleasantries. He was miserable.

Following the meal his mother presented her gift to the Takamotos who, in an outpouring of Western informality, opened it on the spot. Their pleasure was expressed in a toast to his father's quick recovery and the family's continuing good health. Then Takamoto paused, looked around the table and offered a final toast to a long relationship between the Livingson and Takamoto families.

Jonathan was deeply moved by the sincerity and affection of his words.

Then, as if on cue, a band began playing somewhere behind them on the main deck. Takamoto broke into a pleased smile. "I believe the evening's entertainment has begun." He turned to Naoko. "Why don't you take Jonathan-*san* on a tour of the ship while I escort your mothers to the dance floor?" he suggested.

Naoko's eyes sparkled. "I would be pleased to, Father." She looked across at Jonathan. "Would you like to see ship, Jonathan-*san*?"

Jonathan held her gaze. "I would be delighted."

Fenton pushed the broken chain-link fence aside and walked slowly toward the weathered building. He had found it at the end of a run down cul-de-sac of warehouses behind a seedy industrial park. The driveway was blocked by a graffiti-covered, rusting, yellow earth mover, so he had pulled off the road and parked in a border of tall weeds in front of the opening in the fence.

He stopped and studied what appeared to be an abandoned warehouse. The address was faded, but it was still legible over a peeling office door: 932, the street address of record for NuTech Services. Fenton kicked a battered oil can out of the way, picked up a large stone and, in frustration, threw it at the rusted metal doors of the building's decaying loading dock. He could hear the crash it made echoing through the broken window directly in front of him. *Shit. Clever boys,* he thought; *a PO Box, an abandoned building and a phone with an answering machine.* Even the name had thrown him off at first. He had had no luck on his initial search for New Tech Services. It was only after he called information and an operator pointed out that the spelling for that number was NuTech that he was able to run the company down. Only the basic information was available: Name, address, phone number, incorporation date, local bank and officers, David Finley and Stanley Wiggins, but it was enough of a bone for the hungry bulldog.

Fenton pushed back through the fence. He climbed into the van and pulled the diagram he had sent Margo out of his briefcase. "Okay," he muttered, "let's see what we've got." He studied the drawing. *Two guys from two companies that are about to merge form a shady paper company on the side.* He took a pen and began to doodle. *What the hell could they be up to,* he wondered.

His train of thought was suddenly interrupted by the chiming of his cell phone. He unclipped it from his belt and snapped it on. "Jennifer, are you okay?" he asked.

"I know I'm not supposed to call unless it's an emergency, but I've got something you should see and I was afraid to e-mail through the SatCom system, and it can't wait until I get home," she said urgently.

Fenton shoved the diagram back into the briefcase and dug his car keys out of his pocket. "Where are you now?"

"I'm outside in the company parking lot; I didn't want to call from the office."

"When can we meet?"

"I can leave in twenty minutes. Everyone is preparing for the shareholder's merger vote tomorrow. Stanley's at the Civic Center and the office is in chaos. I'll never be missed."

Fenton looked at his watch. "Remember the restaurant where you and Jonathan and I met the first time?"

"You mean Hudson's?"

"That's it. I'll meet you there at three o'clock."

"Fent...?" She hesitated, and for the first time her voice wavered.

"Are you alright?"

There was a long pause. "I'm okay. I'll be there at three."

"Jennifer, be careful."

"I will."

Then she clicked off.

Jonathan leaned against the rail and watched the lights of Yokohama slide past in the dark. Naoko had stopped off at the ladies room and he had a small area of the stern deck to himself. Although they had been together since they left the others, they had not been alone. Other than chit-chat there had been no chance to talk as Naoko skillfully guided him through the passengers gathered at the hot tables, bars and dining tables scattered throughout the cabins and various decks of the ship. Their only moments of intimacy came when they brushed against each other while maneuvering through the crowd; then their eyes would meet, she would hint at a smile and he would suddenly be at a loss for words. *God,* he thought, *I hope she suffers fools.*

A passing ship sounded its whistle, a lonesome counterpoint to the cheerful music drifting back from the main deck.

"It is beautiful night, don't you think, Jonathan?" She was standing almost against him, but not quite touching.

"Yes, it is, Naoko." He turned to her. "Are you warm enough?"

She smiled shyly. "Yes, thank you, for this minute."

Jonathan looked back over the water. "You know, when your father introduced you at dinner my heart almost stopped." He turned back to her. "Do you understand what I mean?"

Her smile unfolded and her eyes danced. "Yes, it was big surprise."

"I had no idea that you were Takamoto-*san's* daughter."

"It is confusing. You see, three years after my first father died my mother married Takamoto-*san,* but I kept my first father's family name. So, I am Matsuzawa and my mother and second father are Takamoto." She turned to him. "But, important thing is, I am always Naoko. Do you understand?"

It was all Jonathan could do to resist reaching out for her and wrapping her up in his arms. "Yes. You explained it very well." He smiled gently. "You will always be yourself no matter whose name you have."

Her eyes fluttered. "*Arigatoo gozaimasu.* You are kind man, Jonathan."

"When we had lunch you didn't tell me that you would be coming with your parents tonight."

"I didn't know. Father only called me after I arrived home from work."

"I'm very happy he did."

"So am I. I was so excited." Her eyes found his. "My hope was you would be pleased."

"I am very pleased."

On an impulse, Jonathan reached over and took her hand. It was the first time he had touched her so intimately, and she made no move to resist. They stood that way quietly listening to the sounds of the ship—the deep rhythm of the engines, the sigh of the water rushing past the hull, the music from the dancers floating on the night wind, and he wondered if she could feel the urgent beating of his heart through the tips of his fingers.

Jonathan was the first to speak. "I love the lights on the water. They twinkle like stars." He felt a delicate pressure from her fingers.

"Do you know the story of *Tanabata*, Star Festival?" she asked.

"The name seems familiar but, no, I don't think I do." He returned the gentle pressure.

"It is from old Chinese legend we celebrate in summer. There are two stars who are lovers—Vega the Weaver, and Altair the Herdsman." She pointed up into the night sky.

"But it is so sad. They are separated by *Amanagawa*, Milky Way. But one day each July, on *Tanabata*, they are able to cross *Amanagawa* and be together. We celebrate their happiness by having festivals and writing poems and wishes, which we tie to bamboo poles."

Jonathan was overcome by the poignancy of the moment. "It is a beautiful story. We have one like it in America. It's called Brigadoon, but the lovers must wait one hundred years to be together."

"Oh, how sad is that story. I would not want to wait one hundred years."

"Nor I, Naoko."

"I would rather be Weaver."

"If I were the Herdsman I could not wait a year. I would swim across the *Amanagawa*."

She turned to him. In the dark her eyes expanded before him like the Milky Way.

"Would you do that, Jonathan?"

The ship rolled on a dark swell and she leaned against him. He put his arm around her to steady her and felt the supple warmth of her body and the fragrant embrace of her hair. At that moment he would swim the Pacific Ocean for her.

He was still lost in the plume of her presence when the music of "Joy to the World" came cascading down the wind. *My God, I must be in heaven,* he thought.

"Am I hearing things? Is that 'Joy to the World'?" Jonathan whispered.

Naoko smiled. "Yes, but it's 'Joy to the World Macarena'. It's my mother's favorite dance." She turned in his arm and her eyes held the magic of a child's wish. "Would you like to dance Macarena with me, Jonathan?" She made no attempt to move away.

Jonathan accepted the gift. "I'd love to. I've never danced to a Christmas Carol, especially with an angel." But on this night, on this side of the *Amanagawa*, with this woman, it was the answer to a long-suppressed unspoken prayer.

The cute little blonde slipped out of Landon's arms. "I think we're going to need music for this," she whispered.

Penny crossed the room and inserted a CD into a stereo and adjusted the volume until the "Rites of Spring" filled the room. Then she smiled and began to unbutton her blouse.

"I thought you would like that."

Landon sipped wine. "How did you know I like Vivaldi?"

"I've done my homework." The blouse fell away as she moved closer. "I think you'll like these too." She unclipped her bra as she moved onto his lap. "Why don't you take it off?"

Landon set the wine glass on an end table by the sofa, then carefully peeled away the lace and let it slip down her arms. He took a deep breath. She was right. She was everything to like—firm and round, no bikini lines, just even, sun-splashed California tan. He kissed her neck and reached up for her breasts, but she smiled and gently pushed his hand away.

She put a finger to his lips as if to say, *we have all afternoon,* and reached over and dipped her finger in his glass of wine. Then she turned back to him and slowly darkened her nipples, first one then the other, until they glistened like ripe grapes. When she was satisfied, she leaned forward and placed one in Landon's mouth while her fingers began to loosen his belt and work their way into his trousers. Vivaldi was rising to a crescendo when Landon's cell phone rang.

She pressed against him and her fingers probed deeper. "Don't answer it, Landon," she whispered and moved her other breast into his mouth.

The phone rang again. He pulled back. "I have to answer it," he protested and reached for the phone beside them on the table.

She leaned back but continued to explore with her hands.

"Oh, God," Landon groaned and picked up the phone. "Landon here."

He paused. "No, Peter, I'm fine." He held her hand. "How was Nishikawa?"

He listened intently. "And that was it? He thanked us for our time?" Landon felt a sinking, burning sensation. "And, he'll be back in touch within the week?"

Landon closed his eyes and lay back. He didn't know if it was the emotional crossfire he was caught in, but for the first time that he could remember he was close to tears.

"No, Peter it doesn't look good." He rubbed his forehead. "Yeah, see you tomorrow." He hung up and dropped the phone on the sofa.

"Was it that bad?" she asked.

He nodded.

Penny slowly slipped her hand out of his trousers and tried to smile. "Don't worry, Landon, there'll be another time."

Landon opened his eyes and looked at her. "No, sweetheart, my time may have just run out."

CHAPTER 14

Dear Japanese Nightingale-san,
I must tell you of new wonder in my life.

Naoko sipped her tea from the Burger King cup. She had arrived early at the gallery to compose her e-mail before Yuki arrived. She glanced at her watch then checked the wall in front of the desk. She was pleased to see that the morning sun had not yet found the circular window above her.

Remember I told you of my new American friend Livingson-san and concern for her husband's health? Well, he is doing ok, but their son came to visit and help with care and now my world is upside down. His name is Jonathan and he came to gallery two days ago and we met each other and had lunch together. Then last night our families went on dinner cruise on Yokohama Bay.

Nightingale-san, my heart is like an orchid blown across Amanagawa by summer wind from Mount Fuji. I feel so close to him, as if he is here with me now. It is because his star burns bright in my heart and I think mine in his. Today he has lunch at hospital with Father and his father, then in afternoon we will go to Fuji Fire Festival on date. But time is short, for tomorrow his father comes from hospital, and then one more day and he will return to his home in America. I feel like ginko leaves scattered before stars. I have not known such a thing before. I know not what to do except let my heart go and trust orchid wind. For such wonder I don't know if I should

thank kami-sama or Elvis Presley. Tell me Nightingale-san, am I okashii (crazy)? Thank you for listening.
   Kokoro wo komete
   Naoko

The sun had entered the window and was creeping across the wall. Naoko took a final sip of tea then carefully read her letter one more time and clicked *Send.*

Margo sighed deeply and opened her eyes. She contemplated the light that intimated the soft curves of her body, until she was satisfied that she had completely returned to her terrestrial launching pad on the Afshar rug beside the Zen incense burner. She carefully unlaced one foot, then the other and with infinite care unfolded from the lotus position. Once on her feet, she slipped into a silk robe and opened the sitting room curtains. When her eyes had adjusted to the afternoon light she walked over to the breakfront where she poured a cup of tea. She picked up Fenton's diagram that Jennifer had given her.

The last hour had been a singularly unproductive cosmic expedition. *Not a sign of the Dragon Lady anywhere. It's as if I keep dialing her number and the phone never rings,* she thought. She turned back to the window and watched as the sun dropped beneath the grove of trees that lined the far edge of the parking lot. *I must be missing something. Either that or the solar flares emanating from Takamoto International are shorting out the frequencies I usually travel. There is definitely something up with Takamoto,* she concluded.

Margo unfolded the diagram and held it to the fading light. From the first moment she saw the cryptic Takamoto notation she had not been able to get it off her mind. What was its connection to InterTel, and did Fenton know of Jonathan's father's association with Takamoto? And was that even the point, or was something else agitating the psychic wind that she was missing? *Maybe it's time to contact Fenton,* she decided, and sat down at the breakfront, closed the desktop and pulled out a sliding shelf that contained a laptop computer. She opened its lid and booted up. Then she entered her e-mail program and was adding Fenton to her address book when the *You Have Mail* button flashed on the screen. She clicked and stared at the announcement that appeared: *jnightingale. Subject: On the Orchid Wind.*

A smile of recognition defined her amazement. "So there you are," she whispered. She double-clicked and the message opened:

The forest of death
A blossom of hope scattered
On the orchid wind

Margo nodded. "Of course," she mused. "Your phone was off the hook. You were calling me, but how did you find my number?" *And, what is the forest of death?* she wondered.

Fenton thumbed carefully through the stack of papers on the table before him. Then he restacked them and went back and examined each one before moving on to the next. Occasionally he would pause and make a note. When he finished, he stacked them face down, then leaned forward and studied Jennifer.

"How did you get these?" he asked quietly.

Jennifer sipped her gin and tonic, looked nervously about the dark restaurant, then edged forward on her seat.

"When you discovered NuTech it rang a bell, but it wasn't until two days ago that I realized why." She set the drink on the table but continued to hold the glass with two hands.

"About six months ago I picked up a new job jacket from Stanley. When I opened it at my desk an invoice fell out. It was from a company called NuTech and was addressed to Stanley Wiggins at SatCom. The invoice was for ten thousand dollars worth of computer imaging services related to a corporate facilities brochure we had produced three months earlier. I thought it was strange, because if there had been any services like that I would have known about it, and as best I could remember, there weren't any." She shifted uneasily in her chair and took a deep breath.

"But I was slammed with deadlines, and besides, it had been okayed by Stanley, so I just stuffed it back in the jacket with my layouts and sent it back to him. I do remember that when the job came back to me later the invoice was gone, but I didn't think any more about it until last week when I was approving graphics invoices. Right there, in the middle of the stack, was another invoice from NuTech."

"Interesting. How much was it for?" Fenton asked.

"This time it was for fifteen thousand dollars and, like the other one, was addressed to Stanley."

"Was it for legitimate services?"

"This time I'm not sure. It was for digital effects for a multi-media show that I didn't work on, but it wouldn't be hard to check out."

"Had Stanley approved it?"

"No, not yet. It had apparently gotten into my invoices by mistake."

"What did you do with it?"

"I gave it back to Mildred along with the ones I had approved. But then a few days later, when you discovered NuTech, I remembered the first one, and that set off alarms."

Fenton nodded. "Go on."

"The billing seemed suspicious, knowing what we now know about NuTech, so I went to Mildred and told her that I was putting together a new budget and was considering NuTech, but I needed to see some of their back invoices to get an idea of their pricing."

"And she bought it?"

"Her only question was, for how many years?"

"I was stunned, but I didn't want to appear too curious, so I just asked for one year."

"Did she say how many years this has been going on?"

"When Mildred brought them to me the next morning she said that if I needed any more to let her know. She had records dating back three years."

"Three years?" Fenton scribbled a notation. "That makes sense. NuTech was incorporated three and a half years ago."

Fenton sorted through the invoices again. "Do you have any idea if these are legitimate?"

"I stayed down last night and compared them with jobs I had worked on." She leaned forward and dropped her voice. "Fent, I was responsible for seventy-five percent of those projects and, with the exception of three jobs, not a single one required the services that NuTech billed for. The exceptions were double billing for services that someone else provided. I know for a fact that those invoices are phony."

Fenton stared at her. "Jennifer, I think you've found the smoking gun. How much money are we talking about?"

Jennifer reached into her pocketbook and handed him an adding machine tape.

He studied the tape, scanning down to the total. "Damn," he said in amazement. "Two hundred and seventy-five thousand dollars. David and Stanley have been busy boys."

"And that only accounts for my seventy-five percent. The rest adds up to another eighty-five thousand."

Fenton shook his head. "And this is for only one year."

"I know. I wonder if they've been doing the same thing to InterTel."

"I think you can count on it."

Jennifer shivered. "Fent, I'm scared. I never thought it would be this big. What if Stanly or David finds out?"

"May I keep these?"

"Yes, they're copies. I made them at Kinko's because our copier has a counter on it. I'll return the originals to Mildred in the morning."

"Good. Not only are they evidence, they're our ace-in-the-hole. As long as I have them, you're safe. In the unlikely event they find out you took them, they won't do anything knowing I have the goods on them."

Fenton reached out and took her hand. "And believe me, Jennifer, if they ever make a move on you I'll put a hurt on them so bad they'll wish they were under the jail."

He could feel the bulldog snorting around and it gave him a rush. In the same instant he became intensely aware of how long it had been since he'd felt the soft warmth of a woman.

Jennifer squeezed his hand. "Thank you, Fent. You make me feel safe."

He caught his breath and attempted to conceal the sudden flush of vulnerability that threatened to undo his display of resurgent bravado.

"What should I do now?" she asked.

He reluctantly released her hand and tried to whip the bulldog back into a lather. "Just lay low and let me take it from here. I know it won't be easy, but go about your job like nothing's happened, especially when you're around Stanley."

Jennifer bit her lip. "You're right, that won't be easy, but I can do it knowing you're there, Fent."

Fenton resisted the sudden impulse to reach out and shelter her in his arms. "And, Jennifer, always, always keep that cell phone with you."

Takamoto smiled and indicated the folder he held in his lap. "I am very impressed with your *Lotus Matrix* proposal, Jonathan."

Jonathan looked questioningly at his father propped up in bed, then back at Takamoto. "My *Lotus Matrix* proposal? I don't believe I understand, sir."

By Japanese standards the hospital room was spacious. Where there would normally be six beds there was only one. Takamoto had insisted that for the sake of comfort and privacy Charles Livingson have a private room. Money was not an issue when Takamoto International's interests and security were at stake, and the hospital had been more than happy to oblige. To Jonathan the room was furnished efficiently in minimalist hospital Zen: three chairs, the bed and a roll-around cabinet supporting a coin operated television set.

His father's translucent cobalt eyes, sheltered beneath silver eyebrows, crinkled when he smiled. Even after five days in bed and gallons of medication, they still had a reassuring twinkle that inspired confidence.

"The *Lotus Matrix* proposal you gave to Landon Tarkington and his Abracadabra project. It was passed on to us as part of a report by Tekeshi Nishikawa, our representative who recently met in Los Angeles with Mr. Tarkington and his partner, Mr. Finch," he explained.

Jonathan was totally baffled. "Dad, I'm afraid I don't see the connection."

Takamoto and his father exchanged glances, then Takamoto nodded. "Perhaps it is time to provide Jonathan with some background."

Charles Livingson studied his son. "Jonathan, what I am about to tell you must remain in confidence. It involves proprietary research, product development and long-range strategic planning for Takamoto International. The overall picture is shared by only a small circle of executives in the company. When I am finished, you will understand why we have decided to include you in this group. Will you agree to that?"

Jonathan considered the import of his father's words, then slowly nodded. "Sure, Dad. Of course I will."

"Good." He gathered his thoughts and continued. "I'm sure that you are aware of the Japanese high-speed cell phone Internet systems. They've been an incredible success over here."

"Yes, I've read about them, and seen kids on the street with their phones glued to their ears and accessing the Internet on the trains."

"One of the reasons it has been so successful is that a traditional computer connection to the Internet is very expensive in Japan. Wireless provides an affordable alternative, plus it's portable. At the moment its greatest acceptance has been in Japan, although similar technologies have been introduced in Europe with mixed results. The limiting factor is that the various systems must be delivered through a telephone company wireless carrier in each country, which requires a multiplicity of players and significant investments in technology, infrastructure and marketing. It is a particular challenge in a country like the U.S., which is already heavily hard-wired to the Internet." He paused and sipped a glass of water.

"Are you with me so far?" he asked.

Jonathan nodded.

"Okay. At Takamoto International we have developed the next generation system, which will bypass national boundaries and be global in reach. We call it Blue Lotus. It is a content-oriented, cell phone Internet service that will be delivered world-wide by satellite. The operative words here are *content*, which includes entertainment, and *satellite*. There have been challenging technological problems to overcome, as you can imagine, but we feel those have been resolved and we are now in the final implementation stage."

Takamoto raised his hand. "Your father is being too modest, as is his way. It is because of his inspiration and leadership as head of our research campus in Yokosuka that we accomplished the technological breakthroughs necessary for Blue Lotus." He smiled. "Forgive my interruption, Charles."

Mr. Livingson chuckled. "You are, as is *your* way, entirely too kind, my friend." He turned back to Jonathan. "Any questions so far?"

Jonathan shook his head. "No, except I still don't understand my connection."

"I'm coming to that." He took another sip of water. "There are two, one direct and one indirect. Takamoto International owns a telephone company named InterTel—"

Jonathan looked up in surprise. "InterTel? That's the telephone company that's merging with SatCom."

"That's right."

"And SatCom owns and operates satellites."

Takamoto nodded. "Ah, Charles, Jonathan is beginning to see the method in our madness," he said with satisfaction.

Jonathan continued, lost in thought. "And, not just any satellites, but communication satellites."

"Right again. InterTel provides our telecommunication infrastructure and SatCom will provide our delivery system, not only for cellular Internet but also for direct satellite television programming. Blue Lotus will allow us to offer a complete home or business communication package, combining the strengths of both media."

"That's absolutely amazing." Jonathan was stunned.

"You understand why I couldn't tell you about our interest in the merger," his father said.

"Of course. But, why are you telling me now?"

"Because of the *Lotus Matrix*," Takamoto answered.

"I'm afraid I still don't understand," Jonathan said.

"Because," his father continued, "we also own Tarkington Productions."

Jonathan stared at him in disbelief. "And Tarkington equals content and entertainment."

His father smiled. "Yes. We can develop a sitcom for TV and spin off the game version and interactive applications onto the wireless cellular Internet—"

"And anybody, anywhere in the world can log on and become a player," Jonathan said with sudden realization.

Takamoto clasped his hands and leaned forward. "Precisely. As you can see, the combination of satellite broadcast and wireless worldwide represents a potentially unlimited market."

His father nodded in agreement. "For the first time the world becomes a truly interactive village."

"That's unbelievable." Jonathan hesitated, processing the significance of what he was being told. "I get the overall picture, but what does that have to do with the *Lotus Matrix?*" he asked.

Charles Livingson held up a copy of the proposal. "It goes without saying that your use of the word *lotus* in the title caught Nishikawa's eye. To say that it was serendipitous would be an understatement, but it was the story and the associated entertainment package that sold it. Jonathan, the *Lotus Matrix* is exactly the entertainment content we were looking for to launch Blue Lotus."

CHAPTER 15

Fenton turned up the collar of the Harris Tweed against the cool nip of the night breeze and sipped his Columbian black as he considered his options. Except for muted sounds from the street and the occasional amorous calls of a marauding band of urban crickets, he had the cafe courtyard to himself. He took a bite of his knockwurst on rye, then hunched forward in the dim light and unfolded his merger diagram. He smoothed it out on the table and studied the drawing, then took a pen from his pocket and backtracked twenty minutes.

Margo's e-mail had come as a shock. He had had no idea who, or what Takamoto International was, much less that Jonathan's father held an important position in the company. All he had known was that InterTel was listed as a wholly owned subsidiary of Takamoto. He was also dumbfounded by the Dragon Lady's latest foray.

"How the hell does she do it?" he muttered. *It's as if she has an inside track on our lives,* he thought. Something about that idea sent up a smoke signal, but before he could get a doodle started it was gone, blown away by the immediate necessity to process the significance of Takamoto. Until now the SatCom-InterTel merger had barely registered on his radar screen, but the new information added to the complexity of the situation, especially in light of the upcoming shareholder's vote. Even at this late date the faintest whiff of impropriety could blow the deal apart, seriously affecting Takamoto International and Charles Livingson, *and* ruin his chances of catching David Finley unprepared. *I'll have to be careful,* he thought.

With Jennifer's discovery of the bogus invoices he had Stanley by the balls. Yet, something about the invoices bothered him. The money wasn't chump change, but it wasn't enough for two guys to make the great escape, especially a high roller like David Finley. And, although they were on NuTech's stationery and had been okayed by Stanley, they provided no direct link to David. If David were confronted he would claim ignorance, and although the circumstantial evidence was compelling, it was not enough. He started to doodle.

Fenton drew a clock with one hand pointed straight down where he scribed the number 60. *The invoices were dated sixty days apart, give or take a couple of days,* he thought. *It's as if they're making a payroll but, as far as I can determine, NuTech has no employees. It makes no sense. What I really need is access to NuTech's bank records.* He pondered his doodle, then drew a smiley face on the clock and the other hand pointed at high noon where he drew a dollar sign. *Time to call in an old favor,* he decided. *But slipping in the back door at NuTech's bank will take time, and it may or may not amount to anything; in the meantime I've got to go with what I've got.* He turned to the merger diagram. Fenton pondered the drawing, then smiled slowly.

"And what I've got is Charles Livingson at Takamoto International," he exclaimed under his breath.

He indicated a check mark by the smiley face, then went to work on the merger diagram. He started by drawing a figure inside the Takamoto International box and labeling it Charles Livingson, then he inscribed a heavy line from the Livingson figure down through the InterTel shape and over to the NuTech triangle that contained Stanley and David. He paused again, then at the end of the line he carefully drew a bold arrow aimed directly at the heart of the David Finley stick figure. Fenton put his pen down and admired his work.

"It's a tangled web, but if I do this right he'll never know what hit him, and anything that turns up at the bank will just add another nail to his coffin," he said with satisfaction.

He opened an appointment calendar, ran his finger over the dates, then checked his watch and calculated the time difference in Japan. *I will just have to be very careful with the timing,* he thought.

The mist shrouding Mount Fuji cast a soft, primordial cloak over the ancient forest that sheltered the Fuji Sengen Shrine. To Jonathan, it felt as if the universe had paused for a breath in the midst of a memory. Even when the sun broke through, its light shimmered with the narrative glaze of centuries, casting whisper shadows of furtive forest *kami* and apparitions of supplicant warlords seeking divine favor on the sacred slopes of Fujisan.

The drumming began slowly, booming through the forest; a heart-cinching rhythm from beyond the dawn of time, from deep in the soul of Konohana-Sakuya Hime, the goddess of the mountain.

"Here come *mikoshi*," Naoko whispered with excitement.

She and Jonathan were standing on the inner edge of an expectant crowd which had gathered along the weathered stone steps and broad entry path leading into the Shrine. Towering above them was a massive red torii gate flanked by two fierce *Komainu*—stone dogs guarding the scarlet portal to the supernatural realm of the spirits.

The drumming grew louder until, from a thicket of cedar trees to the right of the main hall, a procession emerged. Leading the way were two large groups of children dressed in blue and white, striving to maintain their balance as they carried on their shoulders two small portable Shinto shrines in the shape of Mount Fuji.

Following the children was a tree festooned with paper prayers. Behind the tree walked the drummer solemnly pounding the measured, primordial cadence on a large shoulder-borne *taiko* drum. Then, swaying to the visceral rhythm, came the imposing, ornate gold and black mikoshi containing the *kami*. Bearing the divine palanquin were teams of young men dressed in Edo-period costumes decorated in the colors and kanji symbols of their community and professional groups. The shrine dipped as it passed, the gold flashing sparks of sunlight as the grimacing teams strained under the load of the enormous beams supporting its massive weight.

The *mikoshi* was followed by another band of burdened celebrants carrying the *chinkasai*, a larger, more monumental version of the red Fuji shrines carried by the children. Escorting the *mikoshi* and their colorful attendants were Shinto priests, pristine in their white robes and black lacquer hats.

After the *chinkasai* passed, Naoko and Jonathan fell in with the crowd following the procession.

"Fuji Fire Festival is actually two festivals," Naoko explained as they turned from the Shrine entrance into a Fuji Yoshido City street.

"In first part *mikoshi* are carried to community center, then, for second part, big fires and torches are lighted along two kilometers of main city street. It will be like river of fire to celebrate end of Fuji climbing season."

She pointed to a tall structure of wood wrapped with what appeared to be grass matting and fiber rope. "See, there is *taimatsu* ready to burn."

Jonathan was impressed by the sheer height and skillful detail of the *taimatsu*'s construction. "You are right, Naoko. This is going to be very exciting!"

"Wait until we get to Honcho Dori, main street. *Taimatsu* and wood stacked high for big fires everywhere." She gestured with her hands. "There is hardly room to walk."

"I think it will get very hot!" Jonathan exclaimed.

Naoko laughed. "Yes, Jonathan, very hot, like inside of Mount Fuji."

They walked quietly for a minute or so following the distant beat of the drum and enjoying the light-hearted crowd. Suddenly it dawned on Jonathan that he was one of very few westerners in the festive throng. He found it to be a comforting and satisfying feeling.

"Did you enjoy lunch with fathers?" Naoko asked.

"Yes," he replied.

Jonathan wondered how much of her father's plans she was aware of. Remembering his father's admonition of confidence, he decided, that for now, it would be best to avoid business and stick to generalities.

"I like your father very much. Beneath the brilliant innovator and businessman I think he is a gentle man. And, you know, he's quite the internationalist."

Naoko smiled. "I am pleased you hit it off. You are right, he is gentle man, and yes, he thinks of whole world." She looked away as if lost in thought, as if trying to make a decision. After a moment she turned to him.

"Jonathan, have you heard of Black Dragon Society?" she asked cautiously, her dark eyes wide with apprehension.

Jonathan felt a sudden chill, as if the mountain goddess had opened her fan before the sun and cast a dark shadow upon them.

"Yes," he said carefully. "It is a secret society of some sort, I think."

Naoko nodded. "I tell you this so you may understand my father and..." she hesitated, her eyes never leaving his, "...and, me."

She looked about anxiously. *"Koko wa hito ga oosugiru mitai,"* she said nervously.

Jonathan looked at her questioningly.

"It's too crowded here." She smiled weakly. "Come."

Naoko took his hand and led him to the edge of the procession away from the crowd. When they were alone she began slowly, carefully choosing her words.

"Black Dragon Society was formed near 1900 by men who wanted Japan to have war with China. They controlled crime gangs and China opium trade so had very much money. Over years Black Dragons and other secret societies got control of military and many government leaders. When some leaders would not do what they wanted, they would sometimes kill them."

She looked up at Jonathan. "I think there is special English word for such killing."

Jonathan nodded. "Yes, there is. The word is assassinate."

"Yes...assassinate." The word seemed to choke in her throat. After a brief silence, she continued haltingly, her voice taut.

"In nineteen-thirties many leaders were assassinated who were against China war."

She caught her breath. They had slowed their pace and were almost out of the crowd. Jonathan could barely hear the drum in the distance. The afternoon was fading to twilight as the red sun-ball dropped near the horizon. She was still holding firmly to his hand.

"There is a stone wall just ahead. Why don't we sit down and rest," Jonathan suggested.

"Yes, we are almost to Honcho Dori."

They turned toward the edge of the street, pausing to bow to three priests who were blessing the procession.

When they were seated on the stones, Jonathan turned to her. "Who were these secret societies, Naoko?" he asked.

"Many people were from farm country and had old ways. It was time of little money and they were..." she hesitated, searching for the right word. "...suspicious, is word?" she asked.

Jonathan nodded. "Yes, the Japanese word is *utagaibukai.*"

She smiled faintly. "*Arigatoo.* These people were suspicious of business people from city and new democratic idea, so many joined secret societies to keep old ways of samurai."

"I see."

Naoko stared toward the torn remnants of the setting sun and her grip on his hand tightened.

"The Takamoto and Matsuzawa families have been close friends very long time. In nineteen-thirties Takamoto-*san*'s grandfather was leader in industry and my great-grandfather, Matsuzawa-*san*, was leader in government."

She released his hand, opened her pocketbook and took out a small pack of tissues. She pressed open the package and slipped one tissue out. She carefully unfolded it then continued.

"Grandfathers were for democracy and opposed to war and had spoken out against army invasion of Manchuria."

She turned to Jonathan and her eyes clouded. "That year, on night of first snowfall, they were assassinated—Takamoto-*san* at his home and great-grandfather leaving meeting."

Her eyes filled. "Great-grandmother said snow ran red with great-grandfather's blood."

A tear ran down her cheek. She blotted her eyes with the tissue, then turned to Jonathan. "Thought of great-grandfather lying dead in cold snow fills me with such pain I cannot think, Jonathan."

He put his arm around her. The twilight had turned to darkness. The chill he had felt earlier still lingered, but it was no longer just in the air. Now it lodged, like a cold stone, in his heart, its icy weight threatening to drag him beneath the implacable dark waves that he realized had been relentlessly building as she told her story. She leaned stiffly against him and he pulled her close for comfort.

"Nobody knew who did killing, but everybody knew. They came from Black Dragons and Army. Grandparents said they came from 'forest of death'."

She removed another tissue. "It is good it is getting dark." She sat up and dried her eyes.

Jonathan released her and tasted the wet salt of tears closing over him. He struggled for light, reaching for words. "Were the assassins ever caught?" he somehow managed to squeeze out.

"Yes, they were one of extreme plots against government then, but at trial they made patriotic talk and were let go."

Jonathan tried to clear his head. He reached for her hand and the hot anguish of her pain flowed out to him like a merciful angel. The stone melted and he rose to the surface, momentarily free, cleansed in the crucible of their terrible memories. The waves parted and a deep shiver ran through him.

Naoko turned to him, tears replaced by sudden concern. She lifted his hand and pressed it to her heart. "Are you okay Jonathan?" Her eyes searched his through the dark.

He nodded and attempted a smile. "Yes. It was just a chill," he said weakly. The touch of her hand and the healing warmth of her body dispelled the last trace of the darkness. He held her close, her stiffness gone, her head resting against his shoulder.

He took a quiet, deep breath as his head cleared. "That the assassins should escape justice is terrible, Naoko," he said softly.

She continued to grasp his hand to her breast. "Yes, it is way it was."

"Are they still here?" he asked.

"Black Dragons?"

He nodded, newly aware of the intoxicating flutter of her heart against the palm of his hand.

"Yes. They have no power, but said to meet with *Yakuza*, their..." she hesitated, again searching for the correct word. "...Children?"

Jonathan thought for a moment. "Perhaps 'offspring' is the word you're looking for."

Naoko smiled sadly. "It is strange to describe gangsters with such sweet word. You know them by tattoos and missing fingers they cut off."

"They cut off their fingers?"

"Yes, a little at a time to ask forgiveness of *oyabun*, boss, for mistakes they make."

They sat silently in the gathering darkness, momentarily bound by the alchemy of troubling memories, and the sustaining grace of their modest intimacy. Then, after a few moments, Naoko gently released his hand, put the package of tissues back into her pocketbook and looked away toward the main part of town.

"*Mikoshi* will be at community center now. Come, it is time to go. Soon they will light fires."

They stood up and began walking slowly in the direction of the celebration. As they approached the festive throng at the corner of Honcho Dori, Naoko turned to him.

"There is still one more thing to tell, Jonathan."

A group of laughing young people, eating grilled squid and fish on slender wooden skewers, hurried past. When they were gone she continued.

"Takamoto-*san's* father and my grandfather were only boys when their fathers died, but fathers did not shelter them from darkness in world. They studied with them teaching of Buddha. They showed them that some of world is like poison Errand forest where nothing grows but death, never life of fragrant Chandana tree. They taught that they must be like miracle of Chandana tree, and have courage to grow beautiful life even in forest of death. As boys grew, they never forgot fathers' wisdom and taught it to their children." She looked up at him. "I am child of my father. Before he died we walked many days in mountains where he taught me miracle of courage and hope, even if lost in Errand forest, even in death." Her eyes held him. "Jonathan, I hope that even when cold snow and dark side come, I can be Chandana tree, as fragrant as great-grandfather."

They had entered Honcho Dori. Bright booths offering snack food and gifts lined both sides of the street, and all about them in the happy throng stood tall *taimatsu* and stacked wood for the bonfires. High above, a television camera on a crane swung out over the street to cover the pyrrhic festivities.

Jonathan was deeply moved by Naoko's story. "Thank you, Naoko. The story of your great-grandfather is very sad, but he was a brave man who left his children truth and beauty. Yes, I see the Chandana tree in Takamoto-*san*."

Then he took her hand, turned her toward him and gently raised her face.

"And you are more beautiful and fragrant than any tree in the forest."

Her eyes filled with tears, and he pulled her into his arms. They held tightly to each other, then she cried out.

"Oh, Jonathan, look, they're lighting fires!"

All about them flames began to leap up accompanied by cheers from the ecstatic crowd. One after another the *taimatsu* and bonfires ignited, creating a river of fire as far as they could see. It was as if Konohana-Sakuya Hime had folded her fan and allowed the molten heart of the mountain to pour down and incinerate the night. Standing in the midst of the conflagration, Jonathan wasn't sure if the sudden burst of heat came from the fires in the street or the woman in his arms.

CHAPTER 16

Jennifer closed the front door of her loft, locked the deadbolt and set the safety chain. She put the wet umbrella in the antique churn by the door and slipped the computer bag off her shoulder. In the midst of the afternoon commute, a cold front had blown in from Texas, and the wind and rain in the advancing squall line had played havoc with traffic and left her with a chill.

It's strange I didn't get any mail today, she thought. She had stopped by her mail box on the way in, and it had been empty. The letter she had left for the postman to pick up was gone, so he must have been here. *Oh, well.* She shivered, tugged on a sweater from the coat closet, then picked up the computer bag and headed into the kitchen.

She turned on the light and noted the clock over the sink: 5:55. *Time for my daily log-in with Fent,* she thought. She set up the machine on the counter and plugged into the phone jack. While it booted she flipped on the small, counter-top TV by the toaster oven, took a bottle from the refrigerator, and poured a glass of wine. By the time the desktop screen had settled down she was perched on a stool, glass in hand watching the opening titles to the six o'clock news. According to an inter-office memo that had circulated at SatCom that afternoon, an analysis of the impending merger was scheduled for the business segment of the program, and she didn't want to miss it.

Jennifer muted the audio for the opening commercials and turned back to the computer to check her mail. A sip of wine and a click later, her mailbox opened revealing two new messages. She

recognized the first as Fenton's, but it was the second one that caught her eye: *jnightingale. Subject: Stay the course.*
What is this? she wondered, and clicked.

In the night a thief
By his own shadow ensnared
Truth vindicated

Jennifer stared at the message for a full ten seconds before its meaning sunk in. *Oh, my God,* she thought, *somebody knows about David.* She reread the poem a second and a third time and her pulse rate stabilized. *Okay,* her mind raced, *somebody knows, but at least whoever it is doesn't sound hostile.* She took a deep breath and tried to center herself. She reached for the phone, then remembered Fenton's message. She clicked out of *jnightingale* and into *junkdog,* just as David Finley's smiling face appeared on the screen of the tiny TV.

Fenton was backing the van into a parking spot two doors down from the café when his cell phone rang. He squared up by the curb, eased forward and set the handbrake, then turned off the ignition and picked up the phone from the console in the same motion.

"Hi, Jennifer, what's up?" he said.

"Somebody knows," she said tensely.

"Knows what?" he asked. He released his shoulder harness and safety belt and pulled his brief case into his lap.

"But first, the answer to your question is: the merger vote is scheduled for three-thirty tomorrow."

"Then you got my e-mail."

"Yes."

"Thanks, Jennifer." He pulled a pad from the case and made a note. "That's very important. I'll explain later."

"I'll take your word for it," she replied, stress still etching her words.

"Okay." He made a conscious effort to slow down and relax his voice. "Now catch your breath and tell me who knows what?" he said.

He could feel her forcing herself to unwind.

"It was in my e-mail when I got home," she began.

When she had finished reading jnightingale's message, Fenton chuckled.

"I'll be damned. So now the circle's complete. I wondered when she would get around to you."

"What do you mean, get around to me, and who is she? Do you know her?" Jennifer asked. The stress in her voice changed to irritation, then disbelief.

"We call her the Dragon Lady, and the answer to your first concern is yes: she appears to know about damn near everything and everyone. And the answer to your last question is *no*. We don't have a clue who she is."

"Fent, I'm already nervous. I'm sitting here, David's on the news, and now you tell me there's someone called the Dragon Lady who knows all about me and you, and David, and..." She caught her breath. "Fent, I'm not handling this very well—"

"What's David doing on the news?" he interrupted.

"He's being interviewed about the merger."

"Jennifer, didn't I tell you not to let him in your house no matter what the circumstances?"

"Yes, but—"

"No buts. Turn off that TV."

"You're right, Fent." There was a pause. "Okay, it's off."

"That's better, now about the Dragon Lady—"

He was interrupted by the muted sound of a doorbell chime.

"Oh, just a minute, someone's at the front door," Jennifer complained.

"Check before you open it," Fenton instructed.

He could hear her moving toward the front door.

"It's a courier. Hang on, I'm going to put the phone down."

There was the metallic rattle of the safety chain being undone,

137

then the sound of the door opening, followed by muted conversation. After what seemed an eternity, he heard the door close and the chain being replaced.

"I'm back."

"What have you got?" he asked.

"It's an envelope. Just a minute, I'll open it."

There was the sound of tearing paper, then silence.

"What is it Jennifer?"

"Oh God, Fent, it's from David," she whispered.

"What does it say?" he asked and reached for the ignition.

"Sweet Jenny," she read in a shaky voice. "The postman always knocks twice. Check your bedroom."

Fenton turned the ignition key and the old Chevy flat-head six rumbled to life. "Jennifer, don't go in the bedroom until I get there," he commanded.

"No, Fent, I have to see…" her voice trailed off.

Fenton jerked the van backwards, then swerved forward out of the parking spot, barely missing a BMW that screeched to a stop to avoid hitting him.

"Where are you, Jennifer?" he shouted into the phone.

"By the bed." She was barely audible.

He slammed around a corner on a red light. "Keep talking!" The command became a demand.

"All of today's mail is here, spread out on the bed, and there's a photo." Her voice choked. "Oh, my God, Fent, I…I think I'm going to be sick." Her voice choked in a convulsion of terror and revulsion.

Fenton tried to keep his voice calm as the van wheezed and accelerated. "Jennifer, I want you breath deeply, turn around and walk back to the living room and sit down and wait until I get there. I'm only five minutes away. *If this damn thing will hold together long enough*", he added under his breath.

"Yes, Fent, I will," she answered in a strangely detached voice.

I'm going to pack you and Hemingway up and get you out of there; then the next call had better be to Margo, he thought, as he crossed the bridge over the Norfolk and Southern Railroad tracks and headed down the hill toward the Old Carriage Factory.

Martinelli's Bookstore occupied a corner location in a fashionable uptown Atlanta shopping mall. The mall had little appeal to Margo, but Martinelli's was the only large independent bookseller left in town, and she was determined to support it in its battle to stay afloat in the tidal surge of mega-chain book stores that had engulfed the city. She saw it as taking a modest stand for the literary spirit against the juggernaut of mass merchandising. Besides, Martinelli's had the best coffee shop in this corner of the galaxy, *and* it was the scene of her brief encounter with the mysterious Shalimar woman.

In her search for the Dragon Lady, that unexpected meeting had continued to tug at her memory, and since she did not believe in coincidence, and her usual channels of inquiry had turned up nothing, she had returned to the coffee shop on the odd chance of running into her again. She had no idea what to do if the woman was there, except to play it like she always did—let the universe nudge her along and see where it led. She had nothing to lose. *Even if Shalimar doesn't turn up,* she thought, *it's a pleasant evening and I need to get out.*

The bookstore had two entrances. One opened onto the parking lot and the other onto the mall. Margo positioned herself at a table in the coffee shop where she could watch both. On her way through the store she had checked the foreign language and computer sections with no luck. Not a whiff of Shalimar anywhere in the stacks.

She set on the table a bag containing the biscotti she had purchased to take home. She sipped her green tea and unwrapped a bagel. She took her notebook from her shoulder bag and considered the Dragon Lady. *How is she doing it?* she wondered. *How does she get on Jonathan's computer; how does she get our e-mail addresses; and how does she know things before they happen?*

Margo had come to the conclusion that her intentions were benevolent. She still had not picked up any hint of malicious energy, and all her messages had been helpful or at the least playful. She had come to think of her as a benign angel hovering just out of reach, communicating in three-line bursts of poetic insight, just when they seemed to be needed most. *The Haiku form and her pre-knowledge of events in Japan are important,* she thought, but like her identity, its significance escaped her.

"There's something I'm overlooking," Margo acknowledged with frustration. She hated to think that in the Dragon Lady she might have met her match.

She tasted the bagel and checked the store entrances. It was a quiet evening in the mall—very little foot traffic and even less in the store. There were only three other customers in the coffee shop.

Margo thumbed through her notebook and reread the entries from her hacker friends. They had all agreed that it was impossible for a message to be downloaded to Jonathan's computer when he was not online. But one comment caught her eye. One techie had said that when he was baffled by a computer malfunction, he always backtracked and looked for patterns that might have contributed to the problem. *Of course,* she thought, *patterns are my thing, why haven't I picked up on this before?* Margo let the tea warm her. The most obvious pattern was that the Dragon Lady always e-mailed everybody except Jonathan. On Jonathan's computer they always appeared as if by magic when he was not on-line. *Okay,* she thought, *what does that mean?*

"Excuse me."

Her thoughts were interrupted by an attractive young woman standing beside the table.

"Yes?" Margo looked up in surprise.

"I'm sorry to intrude. You look as if you were lost in thought."

Margo smiled. "Oh, that's quite all right. Just lost in space."

The woman returned her smile. "I understand, but I think I may have picked up your bag and you may have picked up mine when we were paying at the cash register." She set a matching Martinelli's Coffee Shop bag on the table next to Margo's. "I think I got your biscotti by mistake."

Margo stared at the bags. They were identical: same size, same

140

color, same logo. It was impossible to tell them apart. She picked up the bag she thought had been hers, opened it and nodded.

"Bran muffins?" she asked.

The woman laughed lightly. "Yes, for a moment I couldn't figure out what had happened; then I saw your bag on the table and remembered we had paid at the same time."

Margo handed her the bag. "It was an easy mistake to make. I'm really glad you caught it. I would have been totally baffled when I got home."

"Thank you. I hope you have a nice evening." The woman smiled one more time and turned away.

"Yes, have a pleasant evening."

But Margo was already back in space coasting on the faintest breath of Shalimar and the night song of a *koto*. When the last note faded, she picked up her pen and slowly wrote: *Only on Jonathan's computer—Identical Bags.*

She sipped her tea and pondered the words, then she slowly nodded and the faintest hint of a smile teased her lips.

"Gotcha," she whispered.

CHAPTER 17

"It was very thoughtful of Maeda-*san* to send my mother and father the gallery's last figurine," Jonathan said. "It meant a great deal to them." He shifted his small backpack and held a tree limb out of the way so Naoko could squeeze between a large boulder and the foliage that nearly blocked the footpath.

"She hoped it would bring happiness to your mother and brighten your father's return from hospital. I was pleased to bring it to them." She ducked under the limb. "Your father looked very well. It was honor to meet him."

"He was delighted to meet you. He agrees with me that you are very pretty."

Naoko blushed. "Oh, Jonathan, *arigatoo gozaimasu.*" Then she smiled. "Father is very handsome."

Jonathan took her hand and helped her up a steep incline and over a large tree root. "Yes, and he seems to get better with age."

They stepped out of a thicket of trees onto a broad shoulder of the ridge they were climbing. The sun was warm and lazy. Below them was a small plot of tilled land cleared from the surrounding forest. It was divided into several gardens separated by rough fences and tall poles. Two weathered sheds broke the tree line on the far side of the clearing, where a man in a broad thatched hat was at work repairing a gate. In the distance, beyond the trees, rose hazy-blue hills anchored by the bright stucco and tiled roofs of the homes and buildings surrounding Yokosuka harbor. To the left was the jade of Tokyo Bay and beyond that the deep indigo of the Pacific Ocean. The only sounds were the occasional call of a solitary crow and the drowsy sing-song of a late cicada.

Jonathan and Naoko stopped to catch their breath. He took a water bottle from the backpack and offered it to her.

"It is beautiful here, Jonathan," she said after she had taken a drink. "How far is it to Buddha?" she asked.

"We are almost there, and from here on the walk is easier. The trail will be pretty level."

"It was sweet of your mother to prepare picnic lunch." She handed the bottle back to him.

He sipped the water. "Yes, it was." He smiled, remembering his mother's attempt to conceal her delight when he brought up his idea of a picnic with Naoko at the Buddha.

He had decided on the flight over that he could not leave Japan without a brief pilgrimage to the ancient Buddha, the birthplace of so many of his youthful dreams. He had planned to go alone after his father returned home and was comfortably settled in. But last night at the Fire Festival, in the heat of the fire and Naoko's embrace, his heart took flight like sparks before the wind. Time was running out. In forty-eight hours he would be on a plane over the Pacific. The irrational fear he had first felt in Kamakura gripped him. *Oh God, I'm lost,* he thought. *Hemingway will just have to forgive me.* There was no other way. He could not leave without seeing her again.

Could she take tomorrow off, and did she have some jeans and hiking shoes? he had asked. They had sidestepped a happy samurai, sake glass in hand, intent on embracing a flaming taimatsu. We can take some food and a bottle of wine, he explained. She had not hesitated. Yes, she had some jeans and a pair of hiking shoes, and she had some vacation days coming. She would open the gallery, then catch the train and be at their house by the time his father arrived home. Somewhere behind them Jonathan had heard squeals of delight as a bonfire collapsed sending an incandescent shower into the night sky.

On the drive back to Kamakura he had held her hand and she had slept with her head on his shoulder. For the first time in five years Jonathan had felt the cool breath of peace.

Now, looking out over the smoky blue mountains, Jonathan felt that gentle hint of peace in the delicate pressure of Naoko's fingers in his hand. He put the bottle back in his pack. "We go this way." He indicated where the trail re-entered the trees to the right of a vertical white trail marker.

"If we are lost we can find way to train station." Naoko laughed when she read the marker.

Jonathan chuckled. "It's true, we're never more than a hop, skip, and a jump from civilization, even up here," he said.

Naoko looked at him quizzically. "Hop, skip, and jump?"

Jonathan grinned. "It comes from a children's game. It means something is close. Like this." And he demonstrated, landing his jump about ten feet in front of her. "See, a hop, skip, and a jump is only this far."

Naoko clapped her hands. "Yes, I want to try."

"Okay, come on. First a hop."

She concentrated then hopped forward on both feet.

"Great. Now skip like I did."

She skipped.

"Now jump."

When she jumped she lost her balance and fell forward. Jonathan caught her and she collapsed against him. They clung to each other laughing, then she looked up and the laughter in her eyes slowly turned to wonder and her lips parted in acceptance. His fingers traced her cheek. Then he lifted her chin and his lips found hers. They were like damp rose petals—fresh, soft and full. He felt them quiver, then she gently pulled away and laid her head on his chest.

"Oh, Jonathan, I like hop, skip and jump," she whispered.

He held her close and caressed her hair. The cicadas filled the forest like a symphony orchestra, and he was sure the farmer could hear his heart pounding down the ridge like a temple drum. They held each other for another moment then gently separated.

"The Buddha is just over the next rise," he said. "It's a little narrow here; you lead the way."

They entered a deep green tunnel formed by the limbs of overarching trees that bent close to the ground, touching the tall shrubs and leafy weeds that formed variegated walls on either side. The smell of the earth was rich with the musky fragrance of humus. Here and there wild flowers, accented by flecks of sunlight floating like fireflies, marked the way. It was as if they had entered an enchanted portal, passing from one world to another.

"I see Buddha!" Naoko exclaimed.

The passageway opened onto a leafy clearing. Tall trees on either side opened to the sky. Scattered about were moss covered boulders that appeared to have been thrust from the core of the earth at the dawn of creation. To the left, shimmering through a window in the trees, was Tokyo Bay, and directly ahead, carved from an enormous, sand-colored outcropping of stone, was the Buddha. It was clad in flowing robes and was seated in an arch, with his legs crossed at the ankles. Beneath its enigmatic smile its right hand rested, palm open, partially raised in a blessing. It seemed as one with the stones and trees, the earth and sea, the hum of cicadas and the conversation of crows. Between its feet someone had placed a container of pink and white flowers.

Jonathan stepped up beside Naoko. They stood silently, momentarily at a loss for words. It was just as he remembered the first time he stood at this spot.

Naoko was the first to speak. "Oh, Jonathan, it is so peaceful. This must be very old place."

"Yes, I think it is very ancient."

They stood in the quiet for another minute, then Jonathan turned and held up a bunch of wildflowers. "I picked these back along the trail." He put one in her hair and offered her the rest. "I thought you should have flowers at lunch."

Naoko's eyes sparkled. "What sweet ideas you have!" she exclaimed with delight.

She smelled the flowers, then studied his face and carefully laced one into his hair behind his ear. When she was satisfied she admired her work and smiled.

"Jonathan, you look very handsome with flower growing in hair."

He laughed, and gently traced the outline of her face. "Let's find a place to eat," he suggested.

They picked a shaded grassy spot beside a large, weathered moss-and-lichen-covered boulder and to the right of the Buddha, where they could look through the trees and see the ocean. Jonathan spread out a blanket; after they were seated, he unwrapped the food his mother had so carefully packed.

"Ummm. It looks like we have an international lunch: American chicken salad sandwiches, Japanese fruit and red bean cakes, and a bottle of Pinot Noir wine from your father's vineyards in France. *Totemo oishii desu.*" He held the bottle up for her inspection.

Naoko slid closer as if to better read the label. They were now only inches apart. "Yes, wine looks very good. Parents think of everything."

Naoko took two glasses from the pack. After Jonathan had uncorked the bottle and poured, she handed one to him. They sipped, then he touched her glass with his.

"*Kanpai*, Naoko," he said softly, his eyes never leaving hers.

"*Kanpai*, Jonathan." Her words floated toward him with the lightness of a butterfly.

Her eyes drew him in and he leaned forward and tasted the wine on her lips. Their free arms reached for each other and he felt her catch her breath as his hand encircled her waist. Then, before he realized what had happened, the words were there, a sigh of joy dancing on their lips.

"I love you, Naoko," he whispered.

Her lips parted and he was enveloped by their sweetness. Then they slipped away and he felt their warmth on his cheek. "No one has ever said that to me, Jonathan," she breathed.

They held each other for several heartbeats, then reluctantly he released her.

Her cheeks were flushed and her eyelashes fluttered. "I think maybe we should eat lunch," she suggested hesitantly.

"That's probably a good idea," he said breathlessly, the revelation of his words beginning to sink in.

They ate and sipped wine between small bits of conversation and stolen glances. Jonathan was in freefall, suspended somewhere between ecstasy and disbelief. When they had finished the sandwiches, he refilled Naoko's glass and then his own. Naoko took his hand and looked into his eyes.

"In Japan we do not use words of love like you do in America. When I said no one has ever said I love you, it is true. Here, I hear your words not with ear, but with heart and hearts speak own language," she said softly. "Do you understand what I try to say, Jonathan?" she asked.

Jonathan took her other hand. "Yes, I think I do, Naoko."

She held his gaze. "My heart tells me that your words are your heart speaking." Her eyes searched his. "Is that true?"

He closed his eyes and lifted her fingers to his lips and listened to the murmur of ancient affirmations imprisoned so long in a heart made dumb by the unspeakable pain of grief and guilt. He kissed each finger and pressed them over his heart as she had done the night before. Then he opened his eyes.

"Yes, Naoko, it is true."

"Oh, Jonathan," she said as he pulled her into his arms.

Her lips found his. "Now I must listen to my heart," she murmured.

Margo opened the drapes and let the morning light transfuse the room. *This time of day is particularly conducive to healing*, she thought. The window faced northwest and at ten o'clock the sun was not yet high enough in the sky to enter directly and create sharply defined shadows. The room was luminous, but edges were soft and accepting. Later in the day she would control the effect with sheer curtains hung on a separate rod behind the drapes.

"Were you able to sleep last night?" she asked, once she was seated in the wing chair facing the love seat.

"Yes, better than I thought I would," Jennifer answered. "Fent insisted on taking me and Hemingway to Jonathan's apartment. It was good to have a safe-house. I wouldn't let him leave, so he slept on the sofa and Hemingway slept with me. I think he was happy to be home and stayed curled up against me all night. He was very comforting." She made a fleeting attempt at a smile.

"How about work today?"

"I called in and talked to Mildred. I told her I had personal business and would be in after lunch. She said not to worry, she'd cover; besides Stanley's at the stockholder's meeting all day."

"Sounds like you, Jonathan and Mildred are a team."

Jennifer nodded. "We call her Mother Goose, but we're really the Three Musketeers. She keeps Stanley in his place and makes it possible for us to do our work. I don't know what we'd do without her."

Margo smiled. "It's good to have a guardian angel." She paused, gathering her thoughts, preparing to enter the twilight zone. "Let's talk about what happened last evening when you got home."

Jennifer shifted uneasily on the love seat and her shoulders tensed. Then the anguish poured out in the form of a confession.

"It was my fault; I didn't push the locksmith to get there sooner, but it was the second time he had been out. The first time I had forgotten to change the lock on the sliding glass doors to the garden. He was coming today to change it."

"Is he still coming?"

"Yes, he's to meet Fent at twelve-thirty."

"Do you think David had a key?"

"There was no sign of forced entry, and when I looked, one of the keys for the sliding glass doors was missing. They were hanging on a ring in the kitchen."

"Jennifer, you realize that you're in no way responsible for this," she said firmly, more as a statement than a question.

Jennifer looked directly at her for the first time. Her eyes were still swollen and red, but in among the fog of fear and exhaustion Margo saw flickering sparks of anger and resolve. *By God, she can do this,* she thought.

"Yes, I know that, but it's still mixed in there with everything else."

"Just as long as you know it," she counseled. Then she opened her notepad and studied her entries from Fenton's phone call the night before.

"Fenton briefly explained what happened and said you had the note and a photo that David left on your bed."

Jennifer nodded grimly, reached into her handbag and took out an envelope. "David is sick, really sick," she said with loathing, and handed it to Margo.

Margo opened the envelope and read the handwritten message, then took out the picture. She stared at it and felt her throat involuntarily choke as she fought nausea. When the initial shock wore off, she looked up. "Is this you?" she asked, trying to maintain a semblance of normalcy in her voice.

Jennifer nodded, fear swimming back to the surface of her eyes.

"Yes," Margo acknowledged, "David Finley is a very, very sick man."

The photo was actually two pictures glued together. The bottom one, the color starting to fade, was of a young girl of about eight with golden curls. The other was a full frontal female nude that had been clipped from a men's magazine. Its head had been cut off and the figure glued on top of the other picture, so that the young girl's head now became the head of the nude torso. The final effect was of a girl-child with a fully mature, nude body. It was obscenely erotic. But what disturbed Margo was its intent. It was clear to her that David's obsession now contained the dark shadows of physical and sexual violence.

"Jennifer, when you were this child was David ever violent toward you or your mother?" she asked with trepidation.

Jennifer crossed her legs tightly. "No, he was always into control, but only since he's returned and I rejected him have I felt it could go beyond that."

"I see."

"What are you suggesting?"

Margo spoke quietly, carefully choosing her words. "I think you're right. As a control junkie, David cannot accept rejection. The idea that you are now the one in control of your life is a threat to his rigid, tightly structured ego, and it may be more than his twisted psyche can handle. This photo is a physical and emotional assault; a desperate, violent, calculated attempt to control you by intimidation. Do you understand what I'm saying?"

Jennifer nodded. "Yes, I do."

"What were your feelings when you first saw the photo?"

Jennifer thought for a moment. "At first I was overcome by shock, then fear, then revulsion, and I just detached. I guess it was to protect myself emotionally, but now, I'm enraged that David could and would invade my life like this. I want to help Fent put him away forever. I'm still apprehensive, because there's no telling what he might do, but the anger is helping me focus on fighting back and getting rid of him. I refuse to let him make me a victim anymore."

Margo saw the fire now in her eyes. "You are very courageous. The anger's a healthy step, but be aware that there's a fine line between you using its energy and it using you. And, be prepared to let it go when you no longer need it, or you run the risk of it consuming you."

Jennifer nodded. "I understand." Then the fires flickered and her eyes misted. "Thanks to you and Fent I think I can do that."

Margo handed her a tissue. "I think you can, too."

She folded the photograph and the note and put them back in the envelope. "I'm sure Fent will want these for possible evidence. If you would like I will keep them for him."

Jennifer looked visibly relieved. "Thank you, I would appreciate that. I don't ever want to see them again."

She looked away and patted her eyes with the tissue. "One minute I think I'm managing, then the next minute I lose it."

"It's going to take some time, but you don't have to deal with this alone. Fent and I are right here, and Jonathan will soon be back."

Jennifer nodded. "I know. The three of you have been wonderful."

When Jennifer had regained her composure, Margo turned to a clean page in her pad. "Now, bring me up to date on Fent. How's he doing?"

She visibly relaxed. "I can't say enough. He's always there. This morning he took me to breakfast and back to the Factory to get my car. Then he followed me here to make sure I arrived okay. It's very nice to be number one on somebody's list." She managed a modest smile for the first time.

Margo acknowledged the smile. "Yes, it is. How are his plans to get David progressing?"

"Last night and this morning were mostly about survival so we didn't talk about it too much, but to say he is aggressively focused would be an understatement; I think it's become personal. The only thing he said was that his plan was proceeding and he hoped to work through Takamoto International once the merger vote was out of the way today."

Margo made a note. "That's interesting. I wonder what the vote has to do with it?"

"I have no idea."

"Will you stay at the Factory tonight?" she asked.

"No, Fent insisted I spend another night at Jonathan's. He doesn't get home until tomorrow."

"I agree with Fent; that's a good idea, and I'm sure Hemingway won't complain."

Jennifer almost laughed. "Jonathan has certainly spoiled that cat. He really hates to sleep alone."

Yes, Margo thought, *there's more to that than you realize.*

"Is there anything else you would like to talk about? If you like you could stay and listen to the music for a while."

"Thank you, but I'm not going to let David keep me a prisoner. I need to get back to work and be busy."

"Then you're all set?"

Jennifer nodded. "One day at a time."

Margo smiled and turned back a page in her notepad. She pondered the thoughts she had jotted down in Martinelli's.

"Before we wind this up, I have one other question. Do you have a laptop computer?" she asked.

"Yes, the company issued one to everyone in the communications department last year."

"Are they all the same?"

"You mean the same brand? I suppose so. Why do you ask?"

Margo nodded and underlined the words *same bags* on the page. She smiled. "Just wondered," she said. Then as an afterthought, "Do you know anyone who speaks Japanese?" she asked.

Jennifer looked at her curiously. "No, I don't think so."

A breath of air was stirring the forest of death, and Margo was sure she had detected a tantalizing hint of Shalimar carried on an orchid wind and the note of a *koto*.

Fenton sat in front of R2D2, sipped his Columbian black and studied his merger diagram. He had added two new figures at the bottom of the page: the stick figure of a man and the stick figure of a woman. He checked his watch and jotted numbers on the page: the present time plus thirteen hours. *It's 4 A.M. in Japan,* he thought. *By the time Jonathan gets the e-mail the merger vote will be history. But, he's got to check his e-mail and talk with his father before he leaves for the airport.*

Time was running out. The events of the last day had added a new sense of urgency to an already pressing situation.

Fenton was convinced that David Finley might be going off the deep end and was potentially dangerous. He wanted to get the son-of-a-bitch soon and, for Jennifer's sake, as discreetly as possible. *When the hammer comes down there must be no connection to her; no possible way that David can ever identify her as a target of revenge,* he thought grimly.

Last night, as he lay awake on Jonathan's couch listening to Jennifer's breathing coming from the bedroom, Fenton realized that in her presence he had come alive for the first time since Mary Beth had thrown away the keys to the Porsche. She was a fresh breath of hope, and he was damned if he was going to let David Finley take that away. He returned to his drawing and carefully drew a line connecting the man and woman, then he forcefully inscribed a bold, defensive barrier around them. He wanted David the hell out of their lives forever.

Fenton took a final sip of coffee and started to open his e-mail program but was interrupted by the flashing *New Mail* icon. He clicked and the subject line appeared: *From: deepthroat. Subject: Bank Report. Damn, that was fast,* he thought. He opened the message and scanned the dozen lines.

"So that's where the money's going," he muttered. *But, why would David be secretly transferring large sums of money to an account in Yokosuka, Japan?* he wondered.

He read the message again. The name of record for the account was Japanese and meant nothing to him, but Yokosuka rang a bell. He stared at the screen lost in thought. Then it struck him. Jonathan was in Yokosuka, and Yokosuka was where Jonathan's father worked for Takamoto International.

Fenton turned to the merger diagram, picked up his pen and wrote Yokosuka next to the Takamoto International box. He considered the relationship of the words, then drew an arrow from David in the NuTech triangle up to Yokosuka, and from there across to Takamoto. He pondered the linkage, then carefully drew a small stick figure inside the Takamoto box at the point of the arrow. He stared at the screen as the significance of the connection sank in.

"Well, I'll be damned," he whispered. Fenton checked his watch. "It's time to kick butt." He clicked on Jonathan's address and started to type.

"It looks like it will be a nice day for flying," Jonathan's mother said brightly. She spooned a heaping pile of scrambled eggs onto a platter, added several slices of bacon, and set it on the table.

The kitchen sparkled with sunlight, reflecting the changed mood of the entire house since his father had returned home. Jonathan put down the *Japan Times* and considered the difference the past few days had made in her. The fatigue was gone from her eyes and the color was back in her cheeks. Both she and his father were back to their usual upbeat, chipper selves. The pacemaker was working like a clock and his father was already showing signs of restlessness from being too long in captivity. He was eager to get back to work. Jonathan had no qualms about leaving them.

"The weather report looks good all the way across. Should be an easy flight," he acknowledged.

His mother turned to the coffeemaker and poured two cups. "How is Naoko? Did she like the chicken salad sandwiches?" she asked, feigning casual interest. "You haven't said much since you got back from the picnic." She placed the cups on the table.

Jonathan smiled. He had wondered how long she could contain her curiosity. "Now, Mom," he chided.

They had returned in the late afternoon and, after Naoko had freshened up, Jonathan had walked with her to the train station. They had walked slowly, trying to extend their time together, attempting to postpone the inevitable. They would brush against each other, their eyes would meet and they would smile and laugh. But as they approached the station, they looked quickly away when their eyes met, and laughs were replaced by pensive smiles and melancholy silences.

They both bought tickets at the station, went through the turnstiles, and climbed the steps to the platform together. Jonathan wasn't sure if he could lift the weight of his heart up the final few steps, but he was determined not to allow his sense of impending loss diminish their last few moments together.

The platform was empty except for two older women and the proprietor of a news kiosk, who was occupied sorting magazines. They let two trains pass as they stood with their arms around each other, attempting light conversation and avoiding the stares of disapproval from the two women. Finally Naoko looked at her watch and turned to him.

"Jonathan, I must get on next train," she said, a tear forming in her eye.

Jonathan surrendered to the inevitable. "I know. It's getting late." He drew her closer. The women turned away.

"You will think of me?" she asked softly.

A train rounded the curve leading into the station.

"Yes, every day. *Kokoro de*—with my heart." He was having difficulty maintaining his composure.

The locomotive burst into the station with a blast of air and the squealing of brakes.

The tear ran down Naoko's face. "You say sweet thing. I, too, will think of you."

The train stopped and the doors hissed open.

Jonathan threw his arms around her. "I love you, Naoko," he shouted over the noise.

The women hurried onto the waiting coach.

She looked into his eyes. "I will listen to my heart, Jonathan."

He released her. "Quick, go now."

She turned and ran for the open door.

"E-mail," he shouted.

She turned after she entered the train.

"Yes, e-mail," she called, as the door closed and the train accelerated out of the station.

Jonathan sipped the coffee. "Naoko is fine. We had a great time." He looked up and caught his mother's eye and smiled, confirming her hopes. "And yes, Mom, we're going to stay in touch. I like her very much."

His mother beamed and fussed with the flower arrangement on the table. "I think she's such a sweet person, and Mrs. Takamoto says she's wonderful in the kitchen."

Jonathan reached forward and took her hand. "It's a very great distance, but we've promised to stay in touch," he said reassuringly. *It is far too early to reveal the depth of my feelings and get her hopes up,* he thought. As it was, everything had happened so fast that he needed to catch his breath and give Naoko a chance to listen to the counsel of her heart. With the perspective of a few hours, he had come to the conclusion that theirs might be her first serious romantic encounter, and she needed time to sort out her feelings. Her artlessness only made her more desirable and stirred his love for her.

Jonathan released his mother's hand. "Is Dad coming down to breakfast?" he asked.

"Yes, he was checking our e-mail when he got a call from Mr. Takamoto. You know they've been waiting to hear the outcome of the merger vote. I do hope it was good news."

"It was great news!" his father exclaimed as he entered the room. "Not even close." He winked at Jonathan. "It looks as if the final piece of the puzzle is in place." He pulled out a chair and sat down in front of the platter of scrambled eggs.

Mrs. Livingson put her arms around his shoulders and kissed him on the cheek. "I'm so pleased." She looked up at Jonathan. "They've worked on this for so long."

"I know. Congratulations, Dad," he said, and raised his orange juice glass in a salute. "And, on top of that you're looking great. It's good to see you up and around again."

"You have no idea how good it feels to be home. I guess hospital food is the same everywhere."

He smiled as he took a serving of eggs but no bacon. "Did you and Naoko have a good time yesterday?" he asked.

"Yes we had a great time. I really enjoy being with her."

"Takamoto-*san* is pleased that you have been getting together. He's mentioned it three times."

"I'm happy to hear that. As I remember, that's not always the case." Jonathan knew that cross-cultural romances were not welcome in some Japanese families.

"Yes, that's very true. But as you've probably guessed, Takeo and Maeko Takamoto are not bound by tradition. They are Japanese of course, but they are also citizens of the world. Oh, I almost forgot. You have an e-mail from someone named Junkdog. Its subject line said urgent.

Jonathan looked up in surprise. "Really? That's Fent. And it says urgent?"

"That's what it says."

"I wonder why he's e-mailing me at your address?" Jonathan wondered aloud.

"Oh, I do hope it's not trouble; Fenton is such a nice boy," his mother said.

"Well, I'm about through eating; I'll take my coffee and go check it." Jonathan placed his napkin on the table and stood up and kissed his mother.

"Thanks for the breakfast. I'll tell Fent you still approve of him."

"What time is Yoshida picking you up for the airport?" his father asked.

"In about two hours, at ten o'clock." Jonathan picked up his coffee mug and started for the door.

His father nodded. "I left the computer on. When you're through with Fenton there's something I'd like to talk over with you. Takamoto-*san* is coming by at nine-thirty and we'd like for you to join us before you leave."

"Sure, Dad. Back in a minute." Jonathan climbed the stairs to the third bedroom his father used as a small office and sat down at the computer. *Whatever Fent has on his mind must be really important to use Mom and Dad's address,* he thought, as he went online and opened their mail program.

It was the only message left in their mailbox. He double clicked on *URGENT* and one line appeared:

couldn't risk missing u. can't talk here. check ur personal email.

This had better be good, Jonathan thought.

Five minutes later Jonathan sat back down at the breakfast table. His father was sitting alone reading the newspaper.

"Where's Mom?" he asked.

"She's out in the garden picking some fresh flowers," his father replied. He folded the paper. "How's Fent?" he asked.

157

"Dad," he hesitated, "we have to talk." The ominous tone of Jonathan's voice dispersed the sunny disposition of the room. His father put down the paper. "Is something wrong?" "I think we should go up to your office where we can be alone." Charles Livingson's crystal blue eyes studied his son, then he nodded. "All right, let's go."

Penny set a glass of carrot juice on the table and opened her pad. "Are you okay, Landon?" she asked. "I haven't seen you since we were ... together, and I was beginning to get worried."

Landon forced a weary smile. "I've been working hard and haven't had a chance to get out, but thanks for asking."

She broke eye contact and looked away. "I was afraid that you might think I was too forward when we were—"

He reached out and touched her hand. "No, it's not that. I've been slammed; eating in at the studio." He groaned. "The food's been killing me."

She seemed relieved and her face brightened. "Then let's see what we can do about that. Tofu burger?"

Landon nodded. "And how about some sliced mango on the side?"

She jotted it on her pad and re-established eye contact. "We need to keep you healthy. Back in a minute." She turned away. The twitch was back.

Landon watched her appreciatively. *That walk is enough to raise the dead,* he thought. He felt his energy level rising. *Maybe there's hope after all. Maybe....* he let the thought die and sipped the juice.

He had told Penny the truth. Since their unconsummated afternoon in her apartment, he had thrown himself at work in an unsuccessful exercise in denial. The agonizing fact was the pain and uncertainty about the company's future was not going away, no matter how much energy he expended running around the studio driving everyone crazy. He had three shows to deliver, and, if they were going to be his swan song, he wanted to go out standing tall. He needed to calm down, recenter, and get back into his natural flow before he went into final production tomorrow. So, twenty minutes ago he had told Ginger to hold his calls and had headed for Papaya Paradise to get back in training. The fact that Penny was on today would just be extra honey on the muffin.

Landon reached into his case and took out a copy of the *Hollywood Reporter*. He scanned the headlines, then flipped slowly through the pages. So far nothing about Tarkington Production's financial problems had hit the press.

"A little treat on the house," Penny said, and placed a bowl of strawberries and yogurt beside the juice. Before he could say anything she was off with an order for the next table.

He mouthed "thanks" when she looked back. She winked, puckered her lips and mouthed "enjoy." His strawberry fantasy was interrupted by Vivaldi being played by his cell phone. The music was a new addition; he had downloaded it just yesterday.

"Landon here." He dipped a strawberry in the yogurt. "Peter, you will be pleased to know that I'm back from the living dead." He tasted the yogurt.

"Oh, really? Kichijiro?" He put the strawberry in the bowl and his voice became cautious. "What did he say?"

He leaned forward listening intently. "Let me see if I've got that straight. Takamoto will fund current production through the end of the season, and development for *The Lotus Matrix*. But that's it. Abracadabra and any other projects are on hold until further notice." Landon pondered the information. "Peter, what do you make of that?"

He remained lost in thought while he listened. "I think you're right. Takamoto's keeping the door open, but just a crack. He nodded. "Yeah, thank God for Jonathan."

Penny delivered the tofu burger and mango, but Landon never looked up. She waited a second then patted him on the shoulder before moving away.

"But something's going on. Why development for only one project? Maybe I'm missing something, but that's not exactly a ringing endorsement."

He nodded, then sighed. "You're right, it's a hell of a lot more than we had yesterday and, given our recent record, is probably more than we deserve."

Landon noticed the burger for the first time and reached for the mustard. "I'll get on the phone with Jonathan as soon as he's back in the country and we'll get moving." He opened the bun. "Let's mount up. We're back in the saddle, amigo."

He clicked off, laid the phone on the table and carefully applied the mustard.

"I hope that was good news." Penny refilled his juice.

Landon looked up with a speculative smile. "Yes, sweetheart, I think it was."

Dear Jonathan,

When you read this you will be great distance across stars over Pacific Ocean. I feel we are like Vega the weaver and Altair the herdsman, on each side of Amanagawa, but close in hearts. Thank you for walk in mountains and wonderful Buddha picnic. It was sweet time for me I never want to end. To get on train was very hard. Father spoke to me this morning. He has great respect for you. I think he is very pleased we find each other. I did not tell him how you spoke from your heart. For this minute it is my secret while I listen to my heart. Please take small gift I send to keep me close.

Kokoro wo komete,

Naoko

Yoshida had handed him the small package and envelope when they had arrived at the airport. "I was instructed to give you this when we arrived at Narita," he had said. "Matsuzawa-*san* was very specific. You are not to open it until you are in the air."

Jonathan untied the raffia bow, then unfolded the gallery wrapping paper and carefully opened the lid of a small box. He reached in and gently removed a diminutive clay sculpture of a female figure sitting on a mountain top gazing into the distance. It fit perfectly into the palm of his hand.

"Oh, my, what a lovely piece." The middle-aged American woman sitting beside him put down her magazine.

"Yes, it is," Jonathan replied. "It's a gift from a Japanese friend."

"It is very special," she observed.

Jonathan traced its shape with his fingers. "Yes, she is," Jonathan said.

"I would say you are a lucky man to inspire such a charming gift."

"Thank you."

"Were you in Japan long?"

"Only a few days; not long enough."

"It's never long enough."

He placed the figure back in its box. From his bag under the seat he took a small leather bound pad he used as a journal and settled back. He had a lot to think about. The woman smiled to herself and went back to her magazine.

He opened the journal and took out the merger diagram Fenton had e-mailed him. After the epiphany of Naoko's gift, it came as a rude reminder of the reality that awaited him.

His father had been shocked when Jonathan told him about David's abuse of Jennifer, but his anger became palpable as he read Fenton's e-mail and studied the merger diagram detailing David's and Stanley's embezzlement of InterTel and SatCom assets and their ultimate destination in a Yokosuka bank account. He agreed with Fenton that the whole thing smelled of corporate espionage.

Charles Livingson's blue eyes had flashed. Such personal behavior and corporate malfeasance was not tolerated at Takamoto, and it damn sure wasn't going to start now. He thanked Jonathan for bringing the matter to his attention, and he got Fenton's e-mail address so their investigative efforts could be coordinated.

Just another day in the forest of death, Jonathan thought, as he folded the diagram and slipped it back in the pad. Knowing his father, and what he had seen of Takamoto, there was no doubt in his mind that David's and Stanley's days of freedom were numbered.

"I'm going to take a pill and see if I can get some sleep," the woman beside him said and turned off her light.

"I took one a few minutes ago," Jonathan replied.

He lay back, closed his eyes and visualized the Buddha. At first he wasn't sure if it was the *kami* or Naoko, but this time he knew he heard the tentative song of heart whispers. He listened, trying to catch the words, but they were indistinct, just out of reach, caught in the hush of the wind. He remained quiet while his heart confirmed their source, then turned the page in his journal and began to write.

"I don't mean to intrude, but are you a poet? I couldn't help but notice," the woman said.

"It's a poem I've been working on for a long time."

"She's a lucky woman," she observed, then adjusted her pillow and closed her eyes.

The sleeping pill was beginning to take effect. "I hope she is," he said drowsily, and settled back in the seat.

The last thoughts Jonathan had before falling asleep were of Naoko in his arms, and the offer their fathers had made to him that morning that could change their lives forever.

Part III

CHAPTER 18

Dear Nightingale-san,
He is gone. It has happen so fast I have no breath. The thought of
us so far apart chills me like winter snow. I am like butterfly lost in
night without stars to guide me. I do not know which way to turn. Is
love bright like shining star one day and cut sharp like sword the
next? If so, I think maybe I am in love.
Naoko

"I am leaving now, Naoko-*san*," Yuki said. She was standing at
the door of the office.

Naoko looked up from the computer. "I am ready to leave also. I
will walk out with you." She clicked *Send*, waited for confirmation,
then turned the machine off. She got up and started for the door.

"Don't forget your jacket."

Naoko stopped. "Oh, yes." She smiled foolishly. "I seem to have
lost my wits."

Yuki smiled gently and turned the lights off as Naoko tugged her
coat on and stepped out the front door onto the sidewalk.

"The stars seem very bright tonight," Yuki said as they stood on
the curb.

"Yes, they are like fire in the sky," Naoko replied.

"In America they say that when you wish on a star your dream
will come true."

Naoko watched as the navigational lights of an airplane flashed a
vivid transit across the glowing heavens. "I like that saying."

They stood silently for another minute, then Yuki turned to go.
"Have a nice evening, Naoko-*san*," she said.

"Thank you Yuki-*san*," Naoko said. "I will see you in the morning."

Fenton turned the envelope over and studied the postmark. "When did you get this?" he asked. The address had been printed by a computer in standard issue Times Roman. There was no return address.

"It was in my morning mail at the office," Jennifer replied matter-of-factly and sipped her iced tea.

"A knockwurst on rye and a chicken salad on wheat?" the kid with the green hair asked.

Fenton looked up. "Thanks, Skywalker. The lady gets the chicken salad."

Skywalker ducked under the umbrella and put the baskets on the wrought iron table. "I'll check back in a few minutes." He smiled appreciatively at Jennifer then headed back into the café.

Fenton picked up on Skywalker's obvious attraction to Jennifer. *It's no wonder,* he thought. *The way the light is playing in her hair it's all I can do to maintain a semblance of dignity.* He hated to admit it, but he had forgotten how nice it was to win male approval for his choice in women, even if it was from a kid with green hair

"I hope the chicken salad is good," he volunteered.

Jennifer sprinkled pepper on the lettuce. "It looks very tasty."

Fenton opened the envelope where Jennifer had sliced it along the top and removed a folded note, a room key and a dried flower.

The note, like the envelope, had been printed in Times Roman: *This Friday 7PM. It's not nice to disappoint Daddy.* The key was for Room 1406 at The Excelsior Hotel in Midtown.

"Nice hotel."

"Nobody ever accused David of having bad taste."

"What's the significance of the iris?" Fenton asked.

"From about the time I was twelve, he would always bring me an iris. It was sort of a signal." She tasted the sandwich.

Fenton pondered the objects, then took out a legal pad and drew a bold arrow toward his drawing of the couple in the circle.

"David's forcing the agenda, and we're running out of options. When you don't show up Friday night, he could get nasty. So, unless we can think of something in the next two days, I won't have any choice but to get a restraining order for your protection while I crank up legal proceedings."

Jennifer sighed. "He's still in control."

Fenton nodded. "He's your own personal terrorist."

"Have you heard anything from Jonathan?"

"He replied to my e-mail and said he would present everything to his father before he left, but there's been nothing since."

"When does he get in?"

Fenton looked at his watch. "In a couple of hours, but he won't be worth much. Are you still going back to the Factory tonight?"

Jennifer nodded.

"I'll be happy to stay with you if you like."

She reached across the table and took his hand. "I really appreciate that, but it's something I've got to do alone. Besides, I don't think I'll be hearing from David until after Friday."

Fenton swallowed his disappointment. "I understand, and I agree, you're in the clear for a couple of days. In the meantime, I'll see what I can come up with."

She gently squeezed his hand. "I hope you'll give me a rain check," she said softly. She held his gaze, then suddenly looked at her watch. "I've got to get back. I'm late for a meeting with Mildred. I'll check in after work."

She released his hand and looked at her half-eaten sandwich as she stood up. "Thank you for lunch. The chicken salad was quite good." She laid her napkin on the table. "I just wasn't very hungry."

"I understand," he said, as Jennifer turned and hurried away.

It wasn't until five minutes later, as he was logging on to R2D2, that the significance of her offer of a rain check struck him. "Well, I'll be damned," he said, and a slow smile of comprehension spread across his face.

But he didn't have much time to contemplate the new potential of their relationship. When his home page opened, he had an e-mail waiting from Charles Livingson.

Dear Fenton,

It was good to hear from Jonathan that you are well, although the reason for our conversation was less satisfying. I want to thank you both for bringing to my attention this appalling matter concerning David Finley and Stanley Wiggins. I have spoken this morning with Mr. Takamoto, and I can assure you that we will move expeditiously to investigate your charges and see that justice is done. I trust that we can count on your continued involvement in resolving this situation in both it's investigative and legal aspects. Please let me know what your terms for such a relationship would be.

In the meantime, we are most concerned about the welfare of your client, and Jonathan's friend, and now member of the Takamoto family, Jennifer Mitford. Please keep me informed as to her situation and if I can be of assistance to her in any way.

I look forward to hearing from you.

Sincerely,
Charles Livingson

Fenton printed the letter, made some notes in the margin, then turned back to the screen. He would welcome a relationship with a large corporate client like Takamoto, and he was confident they could work out some mutually acceptable terms, but first things first. He opened the envelope from David that Jennifer had left with him, refigured the Friday day and time for Japan and started typing.

"David, you can kiss your ass goodbye," he chuckled with satisfaction.

Margo sat in the lotus position on the Afshar rug and thumbed through her notepad. It all added up. Running into the woman at Martinelli's was the breakthrough that made sense of everything else. She loved the irony. After hours of cruising the galaxy the answer had been right in front of her all the time. She knew how the Dragon Lady did it; now the only question was the person's identity. She had figured out a way to catch her in the act, but she admired her ingenuity, and had developed a genuine affection for what she sensed was a kindred spirit. So she had decided against deceptive methods. It would be much more satisfying if she could be induced to come forward on her own. Plan B was available if she was unsuccessful and the Lady turned destructive.

Margo walked over to the breakfront and checked her appointment book. She had an hour before Jonathan was due for his debriefing session—plenty of time. She sat down, pulled out the laptop and typed jnightingale's address and then the following:

The coy nightingale
On identical kotos
Many songs to sing.

Sakana Ya Restaurant for dinner tomorrow night at 7:30. Regrets only.

Then she got out her Japanese dictionary and added: *Hajimemashite*—It will be a pleasure to meet you.

Mildred placed several job jackets and a bundle of mail on Jonathan's desk. "I gave my notice today," she whispered.

Jonathan looked up in surprise. "You did what?" he asked in disbelief.

On his fifth attempt Hemingway had finally convinced Jonathan that, jet-lag notwithstanding, further sleep was out of the question. So, after filling the cat's bowl with Tuna-Tenders and soaking in a hot shower, Jonathan dressed, loaded his gym bag and negotiated a soft landing at Starbucks. On caffeine and a prayer he made it from there to the office in time for Mildred's 2:30 mail distribution. Several people had spoken to him on the way in, and Jennifer and

Mildred had greeted him with a hug, but he had the distinct feeling of returning as a stranger in a strange land.

"Mildred," he asked, "did I just hear you say what I thought you said?"

She nodded and leaned closer. "It's not public knowledge yet, but I didn't want you to get it second hand. I wanted you to hear it from me first," she whispered conspiratorially.

Jonathan stared at her, then a slow smile creased his road-weary face. "That's really great. Did you get a good offer?"

"No, there's no offer. I just decided it was time to take the bull by the horns. I'm just leaving."

"That's very courageous." He hesitated. "I don't mean to be too personal, but are you prepared for this?"

She nodded. "If you mean financially, yes. I have enough set aside to last for awhile. I might even retire."

Jonathan thought back to his meetings with his father and Takamoto. "You know, since the merger there's a good chance things might change around here."

"I know, but it's been my experience that the more things change the more they remain the same. It's a big company and I've done all I can do here. Besides, I'm not getting any younger. It's time to stop and listen to my heart."

"And what does your heart say?" he asked tentatively.

"It's time to go."

"How long?"

"Two weeks."

"That's awfully soon. Life won't be the same without you, Mildred." Then Jonathan paused. "Listen, I'm having dinner with Jennifer and a friend tonight. Why don't you join us?"

"That's sweet of you, but I have other plans. Maybe another time; we still have two weeks."

"We'll have to stay in touch."

She gently laid a hand on his shoulder. "We will. Mother Goose never forgets her friends."

Naoko sat at a corner table in the Burger King listening to Barry Manilow and sipping tea. The morning rush had come and gone and, with the exception of one businessman at the counter, she had the small restaurant to herself. The weather forecast had called for morning showers, and, as predicted, the first drops had started to fall as she stepped out of the Kamakura train station.

Barry Manilow was singing something about autumn in New York, as strong gusts of wind swirled the leaves on the sidewalk and splattered rain against the front windows. The day was a melancholy complement to her mood. She watched a woman struggle with her umbrella as she maneuvered through the Burger King's flapping banners and sought refuge inside the front door. She set the cup of tea on the table and took an envelope from her shoulder bag. Jonathan had been gone less than two days and it already seemed like a year. She wondered if the *kami-sama* laughed or cried to comfort a heart in such pain.

She opened the envelope and removed a folded sheet of paper and a drying blossom. The Japanese Nightingale's e-mail had arrived last evening just as she was closing the gallery. This time it was written entirely in English, and she had to refer to her dictionary for a few words to be sure she understood its meaning. She had printed a copy and had been carrying it in her bag along with the flower Jonathan had given her on the picnic. Every now and then she would unfold the message and listen to the affirmations of her heart as she reread the lines.

Dear Naoko-san,
You wonder if love shines like a star and cuts like a sword. Yes, the brighter the star the sharper the sword. It is a mystery that from ecstasy and pain come great hearts, and from great hearts come great loves. Embrace the star and endure the sword, for it is the measure of your love. Naoko, in this floating world, life is fleeting and love elusive. Claim your love. Your heart knows the way.
Kokoro wo komete
The Japanese Nightingale

Naoko read the lines a final time, then picked up Jonathan's flower and held it against her breast. A ray of sunlight found an opening in the grey clouds and sparkled like falling cherry blossoms in the autumn rain. "Thank you Nightingale-*san*," she whispered.

CHAPTER 19

Like an angel in the forest
of death my savior comes.
Crystal hair flashing
light. Stilling the wind,
calming the dark waves,
taking your glove and
breathing on me the sweet,
lotus breath of life.

Death no longer sucks
my juice. Guilt, her whore,
no longer saps my strength.
And you at last are free, and
I, from the wilderness of my
heart, am finally delivered.

Margo looked up from reading the poem and took Jonathan's hand. "You know that storm was never your fault? It even fooled the weather forecasters."

Jonathan nodded. "I know that, but guilt is an unforgiving god. The storm blindsided us, but I always wondered if I had done something differently: if I'd reefed the sail sooner or, after the boat went over, if I'd dived a little deeper..." He paused, reliving that fateful day.

"You know, I'd just given Lisa a ring that morning. We were planning to have dinner with her parents that evening and then leave for Rome the next day."

Margo attempted to conceal her surprise. "You never told me you were engaged."

"We never had a chance to announce it. I thought it would be best for everyone, as well as myself, if I let it go down with the boat."

"Along with your heart."

"I never counted on that."

The afternoon light rendered the sitting room in the liquid tones of a Zen water garden. Clay flute music floated like lilies on the weightless shadows.

They sat quietly, Margo still holding his hand.

"Are these the final verses?" she asked.

He smiled pensively. "Yes, I'm ready to move on."

"Without Lisa?"

"As long as I have Hemingway, Lisa will be close by."

Jonathan thought back to the day he first brought Hemingway home. "Since he is the one possession of hers I chose to keep in my life, I thought he ought to be the first to know, so last night I had a long talk with him and explained that he would have to make room for another woman in my life."

"How did he take it?" she asked.

Jonathan chuckled. "Like a man."

Margo looked back over the poem. "The new woman, is she the angel in the forest of death?"

He nodded. "I met her in Japan. Her name is Naoko Matsuzawa."

"She must be a very special lady."

Jonathan leaned forward. "Margo, she's the answer to a prayer."

She looked up and held his eyes. "Does she love you?"

Jonathan floated with the question. "She wants to, but the western way of expressing love is very new to her, and she's waiting for her heart to give her the go ahead.

"How are you with that?"

"Like a kid with a jar full of lightning bugs."

"If her heart tells her that love is okay, will you be able to let her go in the morning?"

"Every morning for the rest of my life."

She reached out and gently took his other hand. "Then I think it's time to frame the poem."

"Graduation day?" he asked.

"Graduation day," she answered.

She held his hands a moment longer, then sat back and opened her pad.

"Now, what about Abracadabra?" she asked.

Jonathan got up and walked to the window and looked out. He stood listening to the music and watching the afternoon shadows stretch across the parking lot. From somewhere far in the distance he thought he heard the plucking of a *koto* and leaves dancing in the wind.

"Landon's going to be all right," he said.

"I'm more concerned about you," she said.

He turned toward her. "I know, but you needn't be. After talking with Mildred today I made my decision."

Margo studied him carefully, then smiled wistfully and nodded her acceptance. "I'll miss you, Jonathan. When will you be leaving?"

Jonathan smiled. "In three weeks, but I won't be joining Abracadabra. Landon will be working for me."

Jennifer sipped her gin and tonic. "There was a message on my answering machine earlier this afternoon from David," she said quietly.

The conversation around the table in the fern and fountain corner of Hudson's Restaurant came to an abrupt halt. Jonathan put down his drink, but Fenton continued a salsa and chip dip already in progress.

"What did he have to say?" he asked, as the chip completed its roundtrip.

She set her glass on the table and sat back. "You're not going to believe this, but the Friday rendezvous at the hotel is off," she said with relief. "He's been called out of the country and doesn't know when he'll be back."

"Really?" Fenton said with satisfaction and winked at Jonathan. "*If* he comes back."

"*If* he comes back?" She looked questioningly from one to the other.

"We've been at the café since 5:30 this afternoon," Jonathan explained. "Fent and my father have been rearranging David's future."

Fenton leaned forward. "We had to move quickly because of David's plans for you on Friday."

"Fenton," Jennifer prodded. "I'm supposed to be the client, but I seem to be the only one at this table who's out of the loop. What are you two talking about?"

"You're right," he said apologetically.

Fenton reached down beside his chair and took the pad with his notes and diagrams out of his new leather briefcase. He pushed his salad out of the way and opened it on the table.

"Yesterday I sent an e-mail to Charles Livingson outlining David's corporate shenanigans and the urgent nature of the threat David posed to you. I also pointed out the potential public relations disaster for Takamoto if I had to get a restraining order and his behavior became public knowledge, especially following all the recent press about the merger." He took a sip of his Coke. "This afternoon I received his reply."

Fenton consulted his merger diagram. A new arrow had been added starting at the David stick figure in the NuTech triangle and ending at the Takamoto International box. Surrounding the new arrow were hastily scribbled notes enclosed in equally hastily drawn circles all connected by a web of lines.

"The gist of it is that Takamoto has jerked David out of InterTel and reassigned him to their office in Tokyo. The way it was presented to him I'm sure David sees it as a promotion, but in fact it's a way to contain him while the investigation into his activities proceeds."

"So, he's removed as a potential embarrassment to the company and, at the same time, he's removed as a threat to you," Jonathan explained.

Jennifer stared at them. "You mean he really is gone?" she asked cautiously.

Fenton smiled. "He'll be on the eleven-thirty flight to Japan tomorrow morning."

"God, that's wonderful," Jennifer exclaimed. Then a shadow crossed her face. "But, at some point he'll be coming back."

"Not necessarily," Jonathan continued. "Fenton's sources turned up a bank account in Japan into which David has been funneling large chunks of the money he and Stanley have been ripping off from SatCom and InterTel. My father has Takamoto Security working on it, and from the initial reports it appears as if Stanley is about to discover that he's in way over his head."

Fenton turned to another page in his pad. "On top of that, I've discovered two off-shore bank accounts, one registered to NuTech and the other to David. It looks like he may have been trying to pull a fast one on Stanley, which, when we point out David's little shell game to him, should provide sufficient encouragement for him to cooperate with the investigation. Combined with what you've already dug up at SatCom, and what's coming to light at Takamoto, it's safe to say that our two boys are facing some pretty serious criminal charges, not to mention what the IRS is going to do to them. But, from what I've seen, I suspect David will never get out of Japan. However, since I now represent Takamoto International in this unseemly little matter, if he does, I'll see to it that he joins Stanley making license plates at a south Georgia prison farm for a very, very long time."

Jennifer looked at Fenton in dawning disbelief. "Fent, are you telling me that all the years of looking over my shoulder and running from shadows are finally over?"

Fenton reached across the table and took her hand. "Jennifer, you can finally get a peaceful night's sleep. I think it's safe to say that you've seen the last of David Finley."

Margo caught a whiff of Shalimar as Mishi seated her.

"Enjoy your dinner ladies," she said, then turned and fluttered back to her station by the front door.

The two women sat quietly and studied each other. Shalimar provided a barely detectable counterpoint to the delicate *shamisen* background music. Margo smiled. "So, you're the Dragon Lady," she said.

The woman returned her smile. "Sometimes known as the Japanese Nightingale," she replied and sipped her tea.

"And Mother Goose to those who work in her shoe."

Mildred laughed softly. "If the shoe fits I've always chosen to wear it."

"I thought it might be you. In fact, I hoped it would be."

They were interrupted as Yuko arrived to take their order. "Birds of a feather?" Mildred asked after Yuko left.

Margo nodded. "Yes, I would like to think so."

"I don't think Jonathan realizes how often he mentions you. I've looked forward to this day." Mildred paused. "How did you figure it out?"

Margo wiped her hands with the warm *oshiburi* towel Yuko had provided. She found it comforting after the cool night air. Then she folded it and laid it on the table.

"Once I discovered everyone in the department had identical laptop computers, I realized that all someone had to do was exchange their computer for Jonathan's, and as long as the software and data were the same he would never know the difference. So, I had narrowed it down to the office, but I wasn't sure exactly who it was."

Mildred nodded. "I never used mine, which made it a lot easier. The trick was keeping the information on both machines up to date. Once I had Jonathan's basic software and data copied, it was just a matter of staying current on the dates of the files he changed."

"That seems pretty complicated."

"It wasn't as difficult as it sounds. From my cubicle I could see when he used the machine, and he seldom took work home, so a quick search usually turned up any new changes. Then it was simply a matter of copying them and adding the poem. Most of the time I could do it right in the office when he was out."

"Very clever, but why go to all that trouble? Couldn't you have just left him a note?" Margo asked.

"Of course, but I enjoyed the challenge. Besides, a note would have immediately tied the sender to the office, and it was important for the Nightingale to remain anonymous for as long as possible. This was the best way I could think of to get his attention."

"You certainly accomplished that. But for what purpose?"

Mildred hesitated, then opened her pocketbook and took out a photo case. She removed a photograph from the folder and handed it to Margo.

"This is a picture of my husband and daughter fifteen years ago. She would have been twenty-eight the day after tomorrow."

The photo was of a handsome man in blue jeans and a polo shirt. He had a hiking stick in one hand and his other arm around a pretty young girl of about thirteen. She was dressed in shorts and tee shirt, and her flowing blond hair sparkled in the sun. They had on backpacks and were laughing at the camera.

Margo stared at the man. Something about him was familiar. Then it dawned on her. His smile bore a marked resemblance to Jonathan's.

"She is a beautiful girl," Margo said, attempting to cover her dismay.

"Yes," Mildred answered, a stain of sadness coloring her voice. "She died in an automobile accident two days after I took this picture." She grasped her teacup with both hands.

"Her father was driving. They were returning from a camping trip. He dozed off and the car ran off the road and hit a tree. Lisa died at the scene. Tom never recovered from the guilt and grief. He died two years later of a broken heart."

Margo impulsively reached across the table and took Mildred's hand. She did not resist.

"Her name was Lisa?" Margo asked.

"Yes."

Oh, my God, she thought. *I see where this is going.*

"She had the same name as Jonathan's girlfriend who died in the sailboat accident."

179

Mildred nodded.

"And you saw your husband in Jonathan," Margo said quietly.

"I'd lived through the carnage of one broken heart. Jonathan had survived so far, but it's been five years, and his heart was withering."

She smiled softly. "Remember, I'm Mother Goose, I had to do something. It was my way of giving you a little back-up."

Margo released her hand and they sat quietly while Yuko set their salads and *miso* soup on the table. The music changed from *shamisen* to Japanese New Age. When she had departed, Margo returned the photo and refilled Mildred's tea cup.

"I like your perfume. Shalimar is my favorite fragrance."

"I hope it's not too strong. I never wear it at work, only when I go out."

Margo smiled and nodded. "No, it's just right."

Mildred sipped her tea. "How were you planning to find me if I hadn't responded to your e-mail and met you tonight?" Mildred asked.

"That was plan B. I was going to have Jonathan check the computers' serial numbers the next time you switched, then have him compare them with the company's distribution records."

Mildred nodded. "Plan A is so much more enjoyable."

"When did you decide to expand the circle beyond Jonathan?" Margo asked.

"Once I became the Dragon Lady I couldn't resist. I picked up your and Fenton's e-mail addresses from Jonathan's computer. I already had Jennifer's at the office."

"Did you know about Stanley and NuTech?"

"I suspected that Stanley was up to something. I had enough of an overview of our projects to realize that NuTech invoices and services weren't adding up. I was trying to figure out what to do when Fenton stumbled onto it. David Finley was more than I needed to know about."

I'm not going there, Margo thought. *That would be violating client confidentiality.*

She smiled and changed the subject. "You have a good eye," she said. "Jonathan does have a nice ass."

Mildred blushed. "I thought the first poem had to stop him in his tracks. It was also a diversion—who would ever suspect Mother Goose would say something like that?"

"You really got those boys going." Margo chuckled and tasted the soup. "Tell me about the Japanese connection."

"After my husband died, I needed distance, a major change to help me find enough fresh air to restart my life. Japan was about as far away as I could get, so I went through the application process and got a job teaching English in Yokohama."

"How long were you there?"

"My contract was for one year, but I stayed over for another month and traveled. While I was in Yokohama I met the Takamoto and Matsuzawa families and taught their children."

"The Takamoto of Takamoto International?" Margo asked in surprise.

Mildred nodded. "The very same."

"And, Naoko Matsuzawa?"

"Yes, Jonathan's angel in the forest of death. We still e-mail, sometimes twice a week."

"Then you've read the poem?"

Mildred smiled. "It's on his computer."

Margo nodded. "Of course."

"When you e-mailed me you ended it in Japanese," Mildred said, her statement forming a question.

Margo set her chopsticks on her salad bowl and sat back. "Years ago when I was first into Zen, I took a course in Iai-do. The Japanese instructor was very handsome and enormously attractive. One evening after class I invited him over for drinks. The relationship lasted six months, which in those days was a long time for me." She drifted on the memory. "It was nice to revive the interest in Japan when I met Jonathan."

Mildred smiled. "I understand—samurai nights."

"Yes," Margo paused, "samurai nights." Her admiration for this woman was expanding exponentially.

"Did you know Jonathan is leaving SatCom?" Mildred asked.

"Yes, he told me this afternoon. Do you think Naoko is in love with him?"

"Right now she's confused *and* head over heels, but it all depends on whether she has the courage to follow her heart once she sorts it out."

They sipped tea while Yuko replaced their soup bowls with their entrees. "May I get you anything else?" she asked.

Margo smiled. "No thank you, Yuko. I think this is all for now."

Yuko bowed and turned away.

After they had settled into their meal Mildred refilled Margo's tea cup and offered it to her.

"I guess the only question left is whether you're going to blow my cover," she said.

Margo accepted the cup. "I've always felt that life is a little more exciting if you don't have all the answers; if there are some mysteries left to solve."

"I couldn't agree more."

Margo held Mildred's eyes. "Then I propose a toast." She raised her cup. "*Kanpai.* Long live the Dragon Lady. Her secret is safe with me."

Mildred lifted her cup. "*Kanpai.* To the Dragon Ladies." Then she smiled, and the two cups touched. "And samurai nights."

David Finley was impressed. Not only had Takamoto International flown him to Japan first class, but the reception at Narita airport had been flawless. He had been picked out of the passengers clearing customs by a young businessman who introduced himself as Yoshida and whisked through the crowd to a black Mercedes limousine waiting at the curb. The sun was shining, the air was crisp, and despite the flush of fatigue from the long trip, David Finley was on top of the world.

As they approached the limo, another black-suited businessman stepped smartly forward and held the back door open for him, while a third took his bag and placed it in the trunk. He stepped into the back seat and settled into the rich leather seat. David ran his fingers over the supple surface. *Damn,* he thought, *it even smells good.*

Yoshida slipped in behind the steering wheel. Then the man holding David's door closed it and got into the front seat while the man loading his bags closed the trunk, opened the left back door and sat down beside him. It was only when the two were seated that David realized how large they were. The expensive suits seemed to have been tailored to emphasize their muscular frames.

Yoshida started the engine, the door locks snapped shut, and he pulled away from the curb.

"It's good to have you in Japan, Finley-*san*," he said. "May I introduce Hisamatsu-*san* on my right and Nakamura-*san* on your left."

The man in the front seat reached up and turned the rearview mirror so that their eyes met. What David saw in them chilled him.

"It is a pleasure, Finley-*san*," Hisamatsu said in impeccable English.

The man next to David reached out to shake his hand. When he did, David's blood turned to ice. The extended hand was missing two joints of its little finger and, from beneath the immaculate white French cuff, a black tattoo protruded.

"Hajimemashite," Nakamura said softly in Japanese. His eyes held David's in an iron grip.

"How do you do?" David uttered weakly. His stomach rebelled when he felt the mutilated finger slip into the palm of his hand. Nakamura held the handshake for an extra beat and David felt the fingers of his left hand involuntarily knotting into a tight protective ball. *Oh, my God,* he pleaded silently, *what's happening?*

"Hisamatsu-*san* and Nakamura-*san* are from Takamoto security," Yoshida continued, his eyes never leaving the road. "They have some concerns that must be addressed before we arrive at headquarters."

Nakamura smiled again and spread both hands out on his knees. David realized, with a sinking heart, that the first joint of the little finger of his other hand was also missing. At the same instant it dawned on him where this was going.

"Of course," David mumbled, fear beginning to creep up through his solar plexus.

Hisamatsu caught David's eyes in the rearview mirror. "Mr. Finley, we want to know more about your plans to market Blue Lotus technology." His voice was polite, but contained the veiled threat of an undrawn sword.

The fear clutched in David's throat. "Blue Lotus?" he croaked.

Hisamatsu's eyes continued to stalk. "Mr. Finley, we have detained the person you call the Ferret. We also have his bank account, computer, and the disks containing the files he stole by hacking into the Blue Lotus servers."

Nakamura smiled and laid his right hand over David's. "And, as you may have noticed, Mr. Finley, now we also have you," he said in carefully enunciated English.

David's fingers shivered beneath the intimacy of Nakamura's touch, his jaw began pulsing and he broke into a cold sweat.

The police have found the Ferret-*san* to be most cooperative," Hisamatsu continued. "As you may know, in Japan the police respond most favorably to a confession."

Then his eyes drew the sword. "The Ferret-*san* speaks very highly of you, Mr. Finley. He asked that he be remembered to you."

The sword fell. David felt the stump of Nakamura's little finger probing the back of his hand. Terror destroyed his last vestige of dignity and he lost control of his bodily functions.

CHAPTER 20

Dear Jonathan,
I had breakfast with Father this morning and he told me of you coming to work for new company Blue Lotus. He says you will be Vice President of Creative Services. Also you may live some months in Japan and some months in California. I am proud and excited of you. Jonathan, I listen to my heart and talk with Yuki-san. On your computer we want you to go to Kamakura city website your Wednesday at 7:00 (1900). On website click on "City Cam." It is camera on firehouse on Wakamiya Oji Street. Move camera up street to find big white torii gate and zoom to 10X. Look at bottom of gate. Remember 1900 Atlanta, USA time.
   Kokoro wo komete,
   Naoko

Fenton folded the printout and handed it back to Jonathan. "What do you think?" he asked.

"I don't know, but it sounds interesting." Jonathan looked at his watch. "What time do you have?"

Fenton put his mug of Columbian black on the wrought iron table. "Six-thirty and counting."

"You're sure the computer with the nineteen-inch screen will be available?"

"Vincent promised to be off it by five-forty-five." Fenton grinned and checked his watch. "Six-thirty-one."

Jonathan held up his hand. "I know. I'm a little stressed."

"The news from your father was very satisfying. I only wish I

185

could have been there to see David humiliate himself."

Jonathan smiled. "An ex-yakuza can put the fear of God in you. He's going to love the Japanese prison system."

Fenton settled back in his chair and studied his friend. "So, you're really going to do it."

Jonathan sipped his tea. "If you'll be my legal department."

"I don't know much about entertainment law."

"So, you can learn."

"How about Takamoto?"

"They're very impressed with the way you're handling David, Stanley and the NuTech mess. Besides, it's my call, and I'm going to need somebody I can trust."

"And Tarkington Productions?"

"I'm rendezvousing in L.A. with Tekeshi Nishikawa and Hiroshi Yoshida from Japan for a Monday meeting with Landon and Peter. Nishikawa represents finance, Yoshida, management, and I would like you to represent legal. When we're finished we should have the Blue Lotus creative team in place."

"How do you think Landon's going to take it?"

"He'll probably be in shock, but once the dust settles and he sees the potential, he's going to love it. He's never been able to turn down a creative challenge, and this one is huge. You'll need to bring some non-disclosure agreements."

"So I'm going?"

Jonathan smiled. "What else have you got to do?"

"I can't speak Japanese."

"I can't speak legalese."

"Is Hemingway going?"

"To Japan."

"I'd have to get rid of the van."

"Keep it for an escape hatch."

Fenton sat quietly for a moment, then shrugged. "What the hell."

Jonathan smiled. "Right, what the hell."

Fenton reached across the table and they shook hands.

"What time is it, Counselor?" Jonathan asked.

Fenton looked at his watch. "Six-fifty. We'd better get ready."
They pushed back from the table and headed into the café.

Naoko looked nervously at her watch. "It's twenty-five minutes after seven, we'd better hurry, Yuki-*san*," she called out to Yuki, who was carrying the other end of a long roll of paper and bamboo.

"We are almost there," Yuki called back, as she maneuvered along the crowded sidewalk.

Just ahead, towering over Wakamiya Oji Street were the columns and cross members of a massive, white torii gate. Further ahead on the left was a McDonalds and beyond that stood the firehouse.

"I think we should cross here," Yuki said, indicating the cross walk that that led past the base of the gate.

At this point the street widened and split lanes, creating a large island in which the gate stood. They waited for a break in the traffic, then hurried across with their cumbersome package. Once safely on the island they stopped to catch their breath and put their load down.

Yuki checked her watch. "We made it, Naoko-*san*, with ten minutes to spare," she exclaimed.

"Yes, but I think we should roll it out and be ready. Jonathan's watch may not be set the same as mine."

"I agree. Are you sure he got your e-mail?" Yuki began unrolling the package on the pavement beneath the arch.

"Yes. He was very curious. He said he would go where he could use a large screen computer to see better."

They continued to unroll the paper until it was almost the width of the gate. On either end were attached long bamboo poles that extended down five feet below the bottom edge of the paper.

"I forget how big it is," Naoko said.

A couple passing by stopped to stare at them, then hurried on.

"They must think we are crazy."

Yuki laughed. "They probably think we're demonstrators. This reminds me of old days in California."

"Do you think they will call the police?" Naoko asked.

"If they do, we will be gone before they arrive."

"It is a good thing the wind isn't blowing or we would end up at Mount Fuji."

Naoko checked her watch a final time. "It is time, Yuki-*san*."

They picked up the poles and slowly raised their creation until it was framed by the columns of the torii gate.

Jonathan sat before the computer in Victor's office and logged onto the Kamakura website.

"What time is it?" he asked Fenton.

Fenton smiled. "Three minutes to go," he said and leaned over Jonathan's shoulder for a better view.

"High-speed connections are great," Jonathan said, as the Kamakura website popped on the screen.

"There's the *City Cam* button," Fenton said, pointing at the top of the screen.

Jonathan moved the cursor to a camera icon and clicked. Immediately a wide angle image of the Kamakura skyline appeared. In the foreground was the roof of a building. Directly ahead was a street disappearing into the town proper, all of which were framed by rolling green hills in the distance, and by a beach and ocean on the left. Arrows were on the left and right of the screen with instruction for panning. To the right were directions for selecting a target and zooming in or out.

"According to my map that's Wakamiya Oji Street, and there in the distance is what appears to be the white torii gate," Jonathan said.

He moved the frame cursor to enclose the area of the gate, selected zoom level *2X* and clicked. The screen area enlarged revealing the white gate.

"That's definitely it," Fenton said. "But it's still pretty far away. Try max zoom, number ten."

Jonathan adjusted the camera position and clicked *10X*.

"Look at that," Fenton exclaimed.

The top of the gate filled the screen.

"I'm a little high, let me see if I can tilt down." Jonathan clicked on the frame cursor and dragged it down. As he did, the bottom of the gate and the island came into view.

"I see two people, I think they're women," Fenton said.

As they watched, the two figures bent over and picked up what appeared to be poles and began to raise them into the air. Stretched between the poles was an enormous banner that caught the morning sun as it filled out and rose into its final position.

Jonathan stared at the screen. "Well I'll be damned," he said in amazement.

Painted on the banner was a field of stars with the word *Amanagawa*. In the middle was a heart with two figures. And, across the bottom in giant letters was inscribed: *I Love You, Jonathan.*

He watched until the two figures lowered the banner and rolled it up. Then one figure walked away and the other stood alone in the middle of the arch and waved. After a minute she turned and joined the other figure. They picked up their bundled banner and walked out of the picture.

"I think she's made her decision," Fenton said.

Jonathan floated in a field of bursting stars for another moment before he attempted to answer.

"Yeah, Fent, I think she has."

Then he reluctantly reached down through the *Amanagawa* firmament to earth and clicked the *Exit* button.

CHAPTER 21

Forty-five minutes after Jonathan signed off the Kamakura website, Hemingway greeted him as he squeezed through the door of their apartment with his gym bag and two sacks of groceries.

"These are for you," he said, holding up a bag of Tuna Tenders. "You get an early start. Fent, Jennifer and Margo will be over soon." He unloaded the sacks and put two bottles of champagne, a six-pack of Cokes and a container of dip in the refrigerator. Then he set on the dining room table a bag of chips and a box of deli crackers, along with a ball of cheese and a couple of bowls.

The party had been hastily organized before he left the café. He was still riding a wave of euphoria following Naoko's dramatic declaration of love, and the last thing he wanted was to spend the evening alone. With her proclamation, and Fenton's agreement to join Blue Lotus, and David under lock and key, there was much to celebrate. But before the others arrived he needed to hear Naoko's voice.

She should be back at the gallery by now, he thought. He unzipped the gym bag and put the computer on the counter next to the phone. The gallery phone number and e-mail address were in his browser address book, so he opened the lid, booted up and the desktop screen appeared.

In its now customary location next to the *My Documents* folder was a new file entitled: *Tiger, Tiger, Burning Bright.*

He stared at the glowing icon for what seemed and an eternity, then took a deep breath and clicked.

The Nightingale sings
Her final song. The tiger
Roars. Lost courage found.

Sayonara,
The Dragon Lady

Jonathan let the meaning of the words sink in. *So, it's over,* he thought. "Damn, I'll miss you," he said softly.

He read the poem one final time, then scooped Hemingway into his lap, clicked on his address book and dialed Japan.

Printed in the United States
30290LVS00002B/301-306